STRAY DOGS

Interviews with Working-Class Writers

STRAY DOGS

Interviews with Working-Class Writers

EDITED BY
DANIEL M. MENDOZA

First Edition: October 2016

Down & Out Books
3959 Van Dyke Rd, Ste. 265
Lutz, FL 33558
www.DownAndOutBooks.com

Cover design by JT Lindroos

ISBN: 1-943402-50-7
ISBN-13: 978-1-943402-50-2

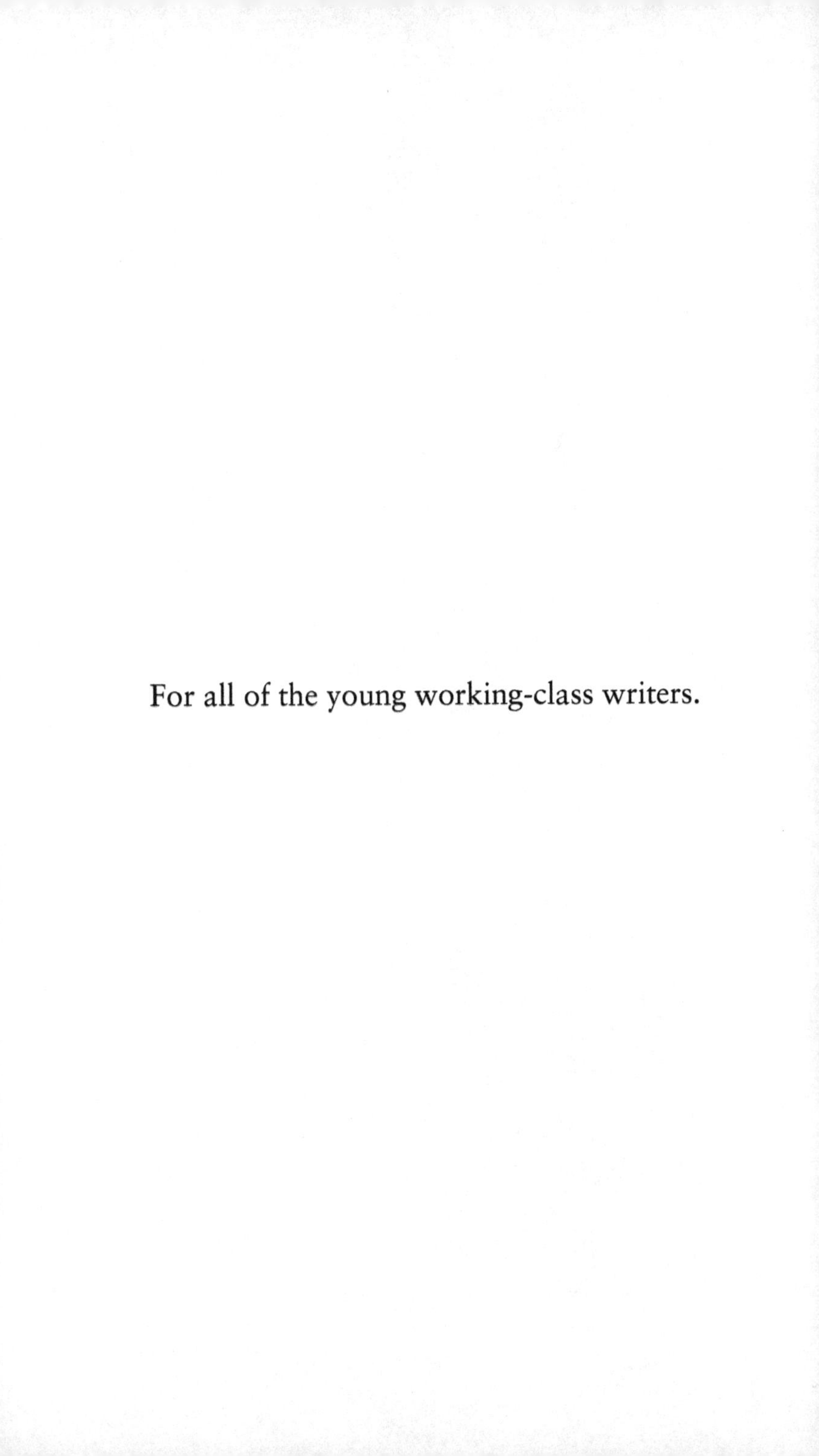

For all of the young working-class writers.

CONTENTS

CONTENTS

Introduction

Daniel M. Mendoza

This has all been a selfish act. It is rare that a young man gets to interview all of his idols, that he gets to ask them all the questions he wants answers to, but that is what I have done here. I can think of no better way for a young writer to begin his writing life than in the way this collection has allowed.

It is my opinion that the writers gathered together in this interview collection are some of the best in contemporary literary fiction. I admit making such a claim in the overcrowded literary period that we live in today is difficult to prove. Today there are more books being published than ever before and many of them come with a support group of literary journals (both print and online) to praise them. A significant amount of these books are written by MFA graduates and many of them are short story collections in the Realist genre. Indeed, to say that a particular group of writers is better than the rest requires some explanation.

I say these writers are the best because they have managed the kind of synthesis that the majority of Realist writers have not. Most Realist writers are stuck in what many call the nineteenth century model of Realism, a style of fiction that has become as formulaic as the tricks of post-modern fiction or the depressed "I" of Confessionalist poetry. When writers borrow from the canonical Realists from Mark Twain to Raymond Carver, they learn to mimic the styles that made fiction by these authors original. When a writer borrows too heavily on the past they will fail to develop their own aesthetic. Most of what comes out of the small presses, which has become the territory for all things literary, mimics traditional Realism. What I find unique about this group of contemporary writers is their experiments with traditional Realism and post-modernism.

Many of the writers have as their central settings and characters a working-class aesthetic. But there is something about the term that bothers me. The literary world, at least the present conception of it, is one that looks down at such titles. To say that a writer is working-class *and* literary seems to be an oddity. Despite the fact that our current age is one that is over with the high theory of post-modernism, we are suffering through the residual effects of it. Many literature departments, for example, are saturated with cultural studies theory, which is a way of looking at art through a cultural-social-political lens as opposed to an aesthetic lens. Our current literary readership, which has close ties to these literature departments, will often regard a working-class writer as one whose primary objective is to comment on the cultural-social-political aspects of the world.

It is rare that a working-class writer of the past has been truly considered an artist. I have in mind a few examples of how associating oneself with the working-class can also mean labeling oneself an outcast in the world of literary art. Today most literary readers would not regard Jack London as literary. Writers like Nelson Algren and Erskine Caldwell are usually passed over for writers like Saul Bellow and John Steinbeck—the last of which is likely to be found in a history class, not a literature class.

Meta-Realism is a term used by Eric Miles Williamson when discussing some Working-Class writers. In Williamson's "Toni Morrison and the School of American Meta-Realism," we read: "The American Meta-Realists tend to be didactic, to write about the destitute, the morose, the downtrodden and the wicked, apt subjects for preaching." He also writes that the words on the pages of these Meta-Realist novels are heavily stylistic: at times "self-consciously deliberate," sometimes "quirky and jolting," or "brilliant and strange," "lush," "stark," "poetic."

These descriptions should come as no surprise once we realize the origins of the most influential in this group. Williamson, George Williams, Steven Gutierrez, JD Smith, and others have either been past students of Donald Barthelme at the University of Houston's Creative Writing program in the '90s; or, they have had an affiliation with the *American Book Review* and Fiction Collective's founder Ronald Sukenick.

It is from these older writers that the Meta-Realists were instructed. But like all great writers they hide their influence well. The influence of Barthelme and Sukenick is difficult to detect because the subject matter of these writers is so different. The Meta-Realists are often called Working-Class Realists because their subject matter concerns several parts of our country that had previously been neglected in most literary realism: the Appalachian south, the Midwest, the Rust Belt, Mexican colonias, ghettoes, and white trash neighborhoods of America. Their characters, which are products of those surroundings, are laborers, alcoholics, drug-addicts, prostitutes, runaways, and in some cases, community college instructors.

Maybe I had first began to notice the influx of working-class fiction when I started sifting through the many review copies sent to the *American Book Review*, where I was an editorial assistant. Many of these were from independent and university presses. Many of them had book jackets that said things like, "The best writer of his generation" or "chronicling the state of contemporary America," which were of course all grossly hyperbolic statements—if you ever want to find something to laugh at while browsing through a bookstore, read the backs of the books under the New Author's section. If you are a writer, reviewer or critic, or just someone who keeps up with literary fiction and poetry in this country, you know that much of the Realist work that is published does not reflect the reality of our times, economically or socially.

To take the working-class as your primary subject matter is a unique one for contemporary literary Realism. When asked to comment on the state of contemporary Realism the writers gathered here will answer that they too are upset with what most authors are doing with the Realist form. But their concern has more to do with the content, not the model. For example, Ron Cooper's response to my question about the state of contemporary American fiction was:

> Big presses get big from selling many books. You can do that primarily by publishing pabulum. How many times can you pick up a novel from a big publishing house and read about another upper-middle class New Yorker needing therapy because somebody hurt their precious feelings or they're worried that Daddy might cut them out of the will? Some small presses publish junk, too, but even the junk tends to be adventurous or about a segment of the population not represented on the best seller lists.

Essayist and poet, JD Smith provided a good anecdote for the disconnect between the big literary presses and readers:

> I am reminded of a story I recently started reading in *The New Yorker*...[b]y the middle of the first column someone had walked

> into a room with a basket of "courgettes."...You don't have to be Bakhtin to know that this word choice indicated the story was by, for, and about a very narrow slice of the American population. I didn't finish the story. This speaks to the larger disconnect between academic and publishing culture and potential readers who are left out in the cold.

If literary Realism is supposed to create a world that informs the one that its readers live in, then subject matter is as important now as it ever was. To insist that the novel being published by the big presses is the highest form of literary Realism is to do what every other American establishment has done with this country: ignore the reality of the working-class. From this you could gather that what the working-class writers are doing is a political act. Again, this was a sentiment that resonated through many of the authors I interviewed. For instance, Juan Ochoa's opinion was:

> I think Mexican-American authors need to break away from the "I'm a poor Mexican, please love me anyway" story and get down to the business of freeing our people. We have a drug war to stop. Our kids are being taken from us and put in foster care because of a draconian marijuana prohibition policy. Walls are literally going up to keep

> people who look like me out of this country. I can't be the only Mexican in America that sees something wrong with all of this.

Patrick Michael Finn's response was just as interesting:

> If writers don't know what the fuck is going on in the world, their writing will ultimately turn out disposable. I suspect there are quite a few writers whose version of staying informed is an hour of "All Things Considered" on the way home from their comfy gigs at the U. I don't hear them yelling about Obama's NSA spying program, for instance. Lots of complicit, well-meaning white liberals out there are churning out books, as far as I can see.

Take a look at presses like Crab Orchard Press and Press 53 or the fiction and poetry that is published in the top five journals in this country and you'll find work that speaks to a readership that is more graduate university educated than working-class. So really, Realism for Realist writers, and, more importantly, literary journal editors, means literature with themes that surround upper-class domestic issues and armchair intellectual nods to Nietzsche.

What the working-class writers are doing better

than any other literary movement in this country is writing Realism that matters in an artistic way *and* a didactic way. It has been a long time since writers have done this. When we think of the characters, places, and plots of the books I am talking about, we find that they are each particularly original. Ron Cooper's *Purple Jesus* takes place in the South Carolina Low Country, its main characters Purvis Driggers and Martha Umphlett conspire together to raid an old man's house only to find him dead and poor; Williamson's *Welcome to Oakland* follows T-Bird Murphy as he strikes out on a number of working-class occupations including garbage man and mechanic; Christine Granados's *Brides and Sinners in El Chuco* features a variety of narrators chronicling the Mexican-American experience in El Paso; Michael Gills' novel *Go Love* and the short story collection *Why I Lie* follow two country philosophers and lovers in the lush region of the Arkansas Ozarks; Joseph D. Haske's *North Dixie Highway* takes place in Michigan's Upper Peninsula and follows army veteran Buck Metzger's quest for revenge, or at least an end to a generations' long family feud.

Through these works the illustration of a particular working-class aesthetic and moral becomes vividly apparent. The characters that populate these books do not become the straw dog constructions of writers who prop up their work with political agendas. This is often the problem with traditional American Realists like Steinbeck and Dreiser. Though they may not have failed at creating realistic worlds that brought pleasure to the reader, these novelists certainly failed at developing characters that were realistic and complex.

Writing literary fiction about the working-class presents this unique kind of problem that involves aesthetics and morals. I think of the famous argument between John Gardner and William Gass over Gardner's philosophy of fiction as presented in *On Moral Fiction* and Gass' own thoughts in fiction first defended in *Fiction and the Figures of Life.* High post-modern fiction in this country solved the issue by simply throwing didactics in fiction out the window. Gass was right to insist that fiction be aesthetically superior, to delight in that manner. When he says in the Gass/Gardner debate that a fiction's goal is to "move into a realm where everything is held in suspension," we understand that the world created is then set off into its own development of actions and responses, of which a sense of morals are constructed and observed by the reader as the narrative develops.

In my experience reading the American fiction published after the turn of this century, I have observed that many have not learned much from this important debate. What continues to pass for great literary fiction in this country can be categorized in two major genres: the first is work that is a poor imitation of the post-modern Experimental era; and the second, is the kind of upper-class realist novel that speaks to a certain small aspect of the American readership. The former is most relevant in the work published by experimental presses like Fiction Collective 2 and Dzanc books, whose works may at times be entertaining but never in that lasting way that their predecessors, Sukenick, Federman, and Gass were. The latter are simply traditional novelists who are nostalgic for a time when writers like Cheever and Updike were the most successful of the east coast publishing establishment.

My immersion in literary fiction began when I was an editorial assistant at *American Book Review.* Victoria, Texas, the small town where *American Book Review* is housed, doesn't allow much for a young intellectual to do but read. So, I read. I logged about twenty new books each morning and in the afternoon reviewed drafts of essays and reviews with then-editor David C. Felts. Afterwards, I stayed behind and had my choice of the hundreds of new books that had arrived at the *ABR* office that month. I would clear the editing table and read. Initially I read until about seven in the evening and then went to my small apartment. At home I read through stacks of old editions of the American and English versions of the *Norton Anthology*, complete works of the major fiction and poetry writers of the American Canon, and literary theory books like Eric Auerbach's *Mimesis*, Richard Poirier's *A World Elsewhere: The Place of Style in American Literature*, and Northrop Frye's *Anatomy of Criticism*. At the apartment I usually made a sandwich and read until I fell asleep. But once I realized that nobody really cared whether I stayed at the *ABR* office until the late hours of the night; I figured I would stay until around one in the morning when hired laborers would come to clean the office and wax the floors.

When Jeffrey DiLeo, the editor of *ABR* got word how late I was staying he had a key made for me so I could open up the office in the morning. Now I could start my day reading for a few hours—I usually opened the office around six—and end the day with more reading. My editorial duties became a break from the real work I was doing: familiarizing myself with contemporary fiction. Later, I was given the task of scanning all of the old *ABR* issues into PDFs. It was a job that I would not finish, but I did get to read every single issue of *ABR* from the very beginning when Sukenick featured writers like Barthelme, Federman, and Gass regularly.

It was after this education at *ABR* that I felt confident in reviewing books. Two publishers in particular were publishing books that were similar in content to what I had started reviewing, Texas Review Press and Raw Dog Screaming Press. Through these publishers I eventually found books by Gills, Smith, Richard Burgin, Larry Fondation, Haske—whose book I designed—and Paul Ruffin (Managing Editor of Texas Review Press). Most of these writers were referred to as working-class fiction authors because they were writing about people who lived paycheck-to-paycheck, or worse.

This interview collection came along when I left

ABR and began studying fiction with Williamson in the Texas Rio Grande Valley. I was still reviewing books, but mostly working and trying to figure out what it was that I wanted to write about. *Stray Dogs*, a working-class writers anthology, was being put together and its publication was to coincide with the authors' meeting at NoirCon in Philadelphia, an arts conference with discussions on the history of Noir literature and film.

Williamson suggested I go with him to NoirCon and meet the rest of this group of working-class writers. The idea of interviewing them came about because of my interest in their work, how they went about creating it, and how it spoke to many readers like myself who found it difficult balancing their artistic aspirations with their working-class background. It also came about because with the exception of knowing Williamson and Haske at the time I hadn't really known many of the other published writers in the group. Interviewing them would give me a chance to avoid small talk and get right into asking them questions I wanted to know about their work, which would hopefully provide some further guidance for my goal in becoming a better reader and critic.

Williamson would be delivering the keynote speech at NoirCon, and Haske, Gills, Finn, Cooper, and William Hastings would be on a panel discussing working-class fiction and its relationship to the Noir genre. I had no obligation but to hang around and ask them questions about their work. So I did.

We met at bars where I tried to differentiate their voices from all the other people laughing and shouting at bartenders, all the while pushing my tape recorder closer to their side of the bar table, or scribbling their responses in short hand. Other times we'd be walking the backstreets late at night in the autumn cold and a single question would strike off a long meditative answer. Some of the initial questions for the interview were done by email if I couldn't get ahold of the writer.

This interview collection really came about by reference: I interviewed the guys at NoirCon and they pointed me in another direction to other writers who would be interested. I figured this would be the best method at getting like-minded writers into the collection. But, there were other writers who either couldn't answer my questions because of time restraints or other projects—on both parts. This collection represents some of the best working-class writers producing work today. There are others, however, like Christine Granados, Dagoberto Gilb, Jodi Angel, and Tim Z. Hernandez who I would have loved to include. Their work would have helped illustrate just how large this genre is, but again, time for this project was a restraint. In interviewing any of the writers I had really only one thought on my mind: what questions are going to help me, a young writer struggling with form, voice, aesthetics, and politics? I say this is all about me and it is. I'm a writer, but I'm late to the game. Many readers, I'm sure are in the same position,

I hope this collection of interviews helps them along the way.

The Literary Merit of Working-Class Fiction

The working-class writer is a strange artist in our politically correct climate. Blacks, Latinos, LGBTQ, and others have voices, but it is rare that the working-class is given attention in this conversation of "minority" voices. Granted they are not a racial minority, but they are definitely an underrepresented voice in the literary community—and perhaps the art community at large.

The writers I'm talking about include males, females, minorities, as well as writers from all genders and sexual orientations. They have produced novels, short stories, and novellas since the early 2000s up until our current year. They write books about the working-class, which can be defined by Ron Cooper as books about "real people and real issues that Americans face, with real worries, not just things like their portfolios or investments." Some of the characters include Eric Miles Williamson's T-Bird Murphy, a guniter from Oakland, California; Ron Cooper's Purvis Driggers, a propane deliveryman from the Appalachian Low Country; and, Stephen D. Gutierrez's Steve, a community college instructor from East Los Angeles. Others, however, are absolutely poor, homeless, and degenerate. Michael Gills's Jack Smith from his short story collection *Why I Lie* is one example. Joseph D. Haske's army veteran, Buck Metzger from his novel *North Dixie Highway* is another. Still, some of the major characters are children, like Christine Granados's Lily in the short story "The Bride" and Patrick Michael Finn's orphan black boy, Louis from the short story "For the Sake of His Sorrowful Passion."

These contemporary writers are not just writing about the working-class, but they are *from* the working-class—or in some cases lower-class—and in nearly every case, they are still a part of that class: they are living paycheck-to-paycheck. Now I am not saying that this is a necessary tenet of the working-class writer. I will say, though, that it lends a certain credibility to these working-class writers that is lost when an observational writer chooses his lab rats to be the working-class.

The narratives these working-class authors present are not often uplifting. The reader rarely comes across a story from a working-class author in which there is an obvious, optimistic conclusion. The main characters seldom end up "happily ever after" in any sense. If we take some of the stories I just mentioned as an example we can see a good illustration of this. In Williamson's first novel, *East Bay Grease*, T-Bird Murphy is the main character. *East Bay Grease* is an unconventional coming-of-age-narrative in which T-Bird grows up in Oakland, California amidst an abusive, drunken mother, and a gang of Hell's Angels who use his mother's house as a place for sex and drugs. The narrative is less about T-Bird's attempts to escape the poverty and violence of the East Bay and more so about his desire to find his place within it. The novel ends with T-Bird back where he began one of his first jobs: changing tires with Pop—not his real father, but the man who raised him—at a service station. working-class writers who focus on shorter works are no different. Finn's *From the Darkness Right Under Our Feet* rarely features the kind of overt optimism one may desire to see in the realism about the working-class. The closest in Finn's collection may be "For the Sake of His Sorrowful Passion" whose orphaned Louis meets up with a group of hobos, one of which gives birth. Looking out at a polluted river the father hands Louis a warm beer and asks him to name the child. Louis christens the baby girl, "Lousie." This moment, as moving as it is, is truly heart breaking. In Louis's lending this child his namesake, he has branded her a life similar to Louis's, one of random sexual abuse and deep poverty. This is all an attempt to show a fiction that mirrors the situations many of these characters, had they actually existed, would have faced. It is an attempt at mimesis, a trope common in all great literature.

Admittedly, the poverty and violence presented in the fiction of many of these working-class writers may be difficult for most readers to accept. It is perhaps one reason why as a culture we cannot come to accept their work as a popular one; its attempts at mimesis are rendered too close to reality. Other writers, particularly Phoebe Maltz Bovy and Adam Fleming Petty offer similar observations.

Bovy's article "Where's Literature's Class Diversity," which appeared in the *New Republic*, offers the idea that Americans don't appeal to working-class literature because it doesn't offer the optimism that most readers look for in contemporary fiction. Interestingly, this hunt for optimism can be satisfied not just by fiction with wizards, vampires, and zombies, but with fiction about the upper-class. After acknowledging that more great books should be written about the poor-class, Bovy arrives at this conclusion: "But the rich-but-troubled character isn't going anywhere, because there's something appealing about a situation where life's more usual obstacles are stripped away leaving only the petty or romantic ones." Is the conclusion that Bovy's article arrives at supposed to speak for readers of escapist literature or for readers of literary fiction? Or, are these readerships no longer exclusive? The article's appearance in the *New Republic* and its earlier citations of articles from *Literary Hub* and *Hazlitt* would leave me to believe she is appealing to an audience familiar with and with a preference for the aesthetics of literary fiction. The problem here is that literary fiction, if we still consider it an art should not simply be read for escapist purposes. I don't take issue with Bovy herself, in fact, I appreciate her placing this argument within a larger reading audience, I simply take issue with the concession that the argument makes. Part of literary fiction's great advantages compared to popular/escapist fiction is its ability to challenge the reader's views and assumptions about the world. This idea together with literary realism has been a part of the American tradition of literature since writers like William Dean Howells and Mark Twain began challenging the popular romantic and sentimental novels of their own time.

In his *Electric Literature* article, "Dirty Life and Times the Past, Present, and Future of Working-Class Literature," Petty compares the attention Dirty Realists—like Raymond Carver and Jayne Anne Phillips—received with the attention many contemporary working-class writers receive. He claims their positive reception in the 1980s was based on an authenticity that many readers today cannot appreciate in contemporary literary fiction. Whereas this authenticity in "lacking things" was valued during the 1980s, today we value an authenticity that is identified with "possessing things." His claim in the end is "[t]hose without the means to purchase such talismans are inauthentic and bland." Today, readers who encounter this authenticity of poverty, I would add, may not necessarily find the authors inauthentic or bland as much as disturbing. The content of working-class fiction does not align itself with the common assumption than many read to escape. After all, who wants to escape from one working-class life to another? Further, readers from other classes may not want to be reminded of our country's own lower-classes or perhaps our culture's opinion of them.

Again, doesn't this view of literature speak against one of art's original purposes? What is even more valuable about the fiction of these working-class writers is not so much their attention to reflecting a harsh reality, but their attention to rendering works that achieve a high aesthetic and moral complexity. "Shitty Sheila" a short story from Finn's *From the Darkness Right Under Our Feet* is about one girl's fall into prostitution in Joliet, Illinois. Her original plan, however, was to meet two friends in Chicago, who were now working as strippers. When Sheila is told she only has enough money to get to Joliet from Kentucky she buys the ticket anyway, betting on getting in contact with her friends in Chicago. She never gets in contact with her friends, the last time she calls the number they gave her, the voice on the other end says, "You call here again and I'm coming to chop your goddamn head off" (56). The paragraph I want to point out finds Sheila on her first day broke and homeless in Joliet:

> She went out to the colorless morning only vaguely aware in her searing half-sleep that she was penniless and stranded, the commencement of a three-day wandering during which she ate nothing and barely slept. She tried for roughly an hour to figure something out but when she realized

> there was no solution she quit figuring and just moved, dulled and disordered by the horns of dingy busses and freight trains, by smokestacks sending bulbous clouds of concrete in the already concrete October sky, and by the constant clamor of hissing and steel sounds pounding from the plants and mills along a river she crossed over rusty green bridges several times in her aimlessness.

The paragraph is made up of two long sentences, which reflects the tiring aimlessness of what will be Sheila's three-day commencement into Joliet's violent underbelly. The adjectives do much of the work to render a clear description of Joliet—one that should be particularly accurate to anybody familiar with the old steel towns of the Chicagoland area. The words and phrases "colorless morning," "dingy busses and freight trains," "bulbous clouds of concrete," "concrete October sky," "constant clamor of hissing and steel sounds pounding," and "rusty green bridges" achieve a multidimensional impression of Joliet; they are heavy on the senses and imagination of the reader. The aesthetics' primary achievement, though, is that it shows the contrast between Joliet and the ideal life Sheila imagines at the end of the story. When Sheila is diagnosed with cancer, likely from the Christmas ornaments factory where she worked in Paducan, she reflects on the life that those people who buy the ornaments must have "the warm homes with families and children opening their presents under the trees that sparkled with tinsel and glitter and strings of colored lights like pretty picnic rockets." Much of the aesthetic in Finn's work serves to not only render his character's worlds as originally as possible, but they should also be seen as functioning to inform the moral complexities of the story. In "Shitty Sheila," Finn's descriptions help the reader understand the relativistic morals that exist in a world like Sheila's. The reader understands that Sheila's tragedy is not simply her fall from the working-class to the impoverished, but it is her romanticization of what an upper-class life would be like.

American literary fiction in this new century is as diverse as the people in our country. The current debates about who deserves the attention of our country's readership highlights this, whereas the end of the previous century concerned itself more so with the form of literary fiction. With the proliferation of literary magazines and reviews, both in print and online, I think it's safe to say that literary realism and experimental fiction can exist alongside one another. Perhaps much of the debate in this new century will continue to concern itself with the varying voices of American literary fiction. I add to this that what is necessary to recognize is these varying voices should not only be relegated to the color of one's skin or sexual or gender orientation, but by social class, as well. In light of this acknowledgement, people will find that reading the literary realism of the working-class may offer great insight into the aesthetic and moral experiences of much of our country's citizens.

Working-Class Fiction Symposium
NoirCon, October 2014

William Hastings edited *Stray Dogs*, a collection of working-class fiction published by Down & Out Books. Shortly after the printing date, NoirCon, a conference for Noir literature, film, and art was being held in Philadelphia. The major authors in the *Stray Dogs* anthology were invited to attend and speak in the *Stray Dogs: Writings from the Other America* panel.

I decided it would be a good idea to go to Philadelphia and begin work on an interview collection with the *Stray Dogs* panel and other working-class writers. Of the writers that attended the conference, the following were on the panel: William Hastings, who moderated the panel, Eric Miles Williamson, Michael Gills, Vicki Hendricks, Ron Cooper, Joseph Daniel Haske, and Patrick Michael Finn.

The crowd took a particular interest in this group of writers. In a conversation with Hastings the night before the panel discussion, I asked him what he thought about the Noir genre's attraction to working-class fiction. He said that it was only an obvious interest from the fact that Noir readers see similarities in the novels of working-class fiction writers. Noir has always been about the underbelly of society, but Noir authors are rarely from that underbelly; they are in many ways journalists who record from a distance. Working-class fiction writers are a curiosity to much of the Noir world—and perhaps, the literary world in general—because they are a group of writers who are *from* that dark, impoverished world.

This latter observation was obvious at NoirCon, where every place I looked that weekend in October 2014, people were talking about these "Working-Class writers" or people were in the bars and cafes reading copies of their books. Attendance to listen to the panel was no different; listeners crowded into the little theatre house and sat anxiously to see what these "Stray Dogs" would say.

They weren't disappointed. It began with Williamson sitting down at the table and slamming a brown-bagged bottle of whiskey on the conference table. The crowd hushed. Immediately after, Haske took a swig from it and so began the panel, with the writer's passing the bottle back and forth and talking about literature. This was the first time that all of the writers were gathered together under one roof. I think many of the writers fed off the excitement of hearing each other talk about their favorite books and discuss the social-political implications of writing working-class fiction.

Hastings' questions, though few, were complex enough to hit at the heart of what many of these writers were trying to do either aesthetically or philosophically. What could be most admired from this group of writers on the panel was their honesty to the questions. Often times an author puts on another mask, that of a highly intellectual artist, and his responses, though seemingly complex, are often fluffed to avoid answering the real questions being asked; this was not the case in the "Stray Dogs" panel.

For example, when Hastings asked about the notion of responsibility, the answers were varied and at times confrontational. Some on the panel replied that they have only a responsibility to give a voice to the voiceless poor that they write about. Some thought that the notion of responsibility is not a thing that a writer takes up voluntarily, but it is one that is given to him or her. Others, however, said they could care less about the notion of responsibility in art.

Considering that question alone we can already see that, though these writers share the working-class experience, their philosophies are as varied as their novels. The panel was an engaging conversation for the audience to sit in on, and perhaps it even made for the sale of more books.

William Hastings (WH): There is a whole movement happening in fiction, and it's happening in the literary genre world.

Eric Miles Williamson (EMW): And Barry Hannah.

WH: Yeah, and Larry Brown, these are guys that

have been working with this mentality. This isn't Karen Russell, these guys aren't winning MacArthur awards for writing crap. The thing I noticed is that this movement in the literary magazines is the best of what the Noir writers have been doing all along. As Eric (Williamson) mentioned they are all considered literary realists, but it's getting pegged as Noir, overseas, in France, it's pegged as Noir.

What I like about all of the writers that are up on this panel is that their work is a gross confrontation of how life is lived when the rest of the literary establishment isn't addressing this. They're talking about the work-a-day Americans.

What I'm beginning to think about in light of recent political events, the uprising in Ferguson, in Pennsylvania—the manhunt—is the characters that these guys write about are starting to get very angry, starting to wake up. The middle-classes and the upper-middle classes get angry at the ballot boxes. This is traditionally what happens. But the people who have nothing to lose, these are the people that are starting to hunt officers, that are starting to burn cities.

The first question I have for the panel is, what makes good fiction?

Ron Cooper (RC): Well, if any of you flew in for this conference, or if any of you are going to fly out, take a look at what's on the shelves at the airports. I flew up from Florida, and at the Orlando airport, at the Charlotte airport, and the airport here, I made a point to see what was on the shelves. It's fiction that's been high-jacked by the New York literati for about fifty years, and you don't find the other America being represented on the shelves.

I think that what you can discover is that there are real people writing about real issues that Americans face, with real worries, not just worried about things like their portfolios or investments.

I joke to people that there are other people who are good writers where I'm from. I'm from the low country in South Carolina, and I say those other people's characters are worried about their investments, my characters are worried about hookworm. I had never realized there was literature like that; I didn't start reading until I got to college. I was no literary fan. But I found out that real people could actually be represented by writers.

As Eric said this morning, there is a generation of writers that weren't around in the first half of the century. But there are also a whole bunch of publishers that weren't around either. If you were trying to publish a book in the '60s or the '70s, you had about four people you could send the book to. Now guys like Eric Campbell know there is good stuff out there, and still the New York establishment insists on trying to convince people in this country that John Updike is the kind of stuff that only matters as literature. Other things matter.

Vicki Hendricks (VH): Let me just say that I am

really in my element here, I love it. I think it's why I became a writer. All these male hormones make me want to start trouble. I thought I'd grown out of that.

I was brought up on the classics, not because I was from an educated family, but from school. My first dip into Noir or Naturalism was in my mid-thirties. I found Bukowski. I thought what I liked about him were his central elements: drink, fuck, puke, repeat. But now I'm thinking it was his realistic stuff, things like going after a job, and losing a job, and then starting all over again.

Michael Gills (MG): I'd like to thank my publishers who are here, Raw Dog Screaming Press. They put out a book of mine called *White Indians*, the first line of which is: "My uncle once talked me into pissing onto an electric fence, what a surprise that was."

And you know people put it different ways, when they talk about the idea of great literature. Kafka said good fiction should be like an ax splitting open your heart and letting the cold run out. Emily Dickinson said she knows she reads something good when it feels like it's taken the top of her head off and air is just whizzing over. Good fiction has about it a fire.

EMW: I'm a thief, and the only reason I read books is to steal things from other writers. I read with a red pen so I can steal lines, phrases, paragraphs from other writers. Now, nobody ever catches me, I've only been caught once. In all the reviews of my books, I've only been caught once.

I'll be brief—I sound like Polonius now. I only read to steal from other writers. I believe that there is no personal style; writers don't come out original like Athena from Zeus's head. Everybody steals or learns a writer's style and does the opposite. The best writers are the best anthologists, who steal here, and there, and here and then this combination of their theft becomes their style.

It's fucking true, you ask any author who influences you, and that is who the author is. Of course, we all go back to Homer. And we start branching off from there. Either you're Whitman or Dickinson—if you're an American poet, we only have two poets, everything goes back to them. In twentieth century American fiction it's Hemingway or Faulkner. You write long sentences that are bloated or you write sentences that are grunts, like Hemingway. Or you combine them like Cormac McCarthy. That's the way it works.

Joseph Daniel Haske (JDH): The thing that I really like is aphorisms, everybody on this panel is a lover of aphorism. We might have been misleading that language only comes in one form, like Updike, some are led to believe that his work, his style, is the only kind of aphorism. But it's not; working-class people say brilliant things, and they say it in a unique way.

Patrick Michael Finn (PMF): I know I've read something exceptional when I can't stop thinking about specific lines, sentences, scenes.

RC: Aphorisms! [audience laughs]

PMF: Yeah, there you go, those things are infinitely memorable. There's a scene in McCarthy's *Suttree* where this watermelon fucker is walking around Knoxville in the '60s, and the narrator says something like "The sun like a bunghole to a greater hell beyond."

I love that transformation of a star into a puncture through the sky. I read it when I was living in Tucson, so there were plenty of days for me to say, "Ah, today the sun is like a bunghole," and so forth.

Starting in July and, yesterday, I actually finished it, *2666* by Bolano. There is this great scene, three literary critics are driving around this version of Juarez. The literary critics in the scene are from Europe, and they've never seen the third world and now they just got to Juarez, right on the border of New Mexico. They drive past the soccer field "where a team of the terminally ill was playing against the team of the starving to death." And it's not funny, but I laughed my ass off, and you know, that's what it looked like to these well-fed academics in Europe. It was post-apocalyptic.

One editor said a good story becomes an instant memory. So it doesn't necessarily have to be lines but just colors, moods, atmosphere, that you always associate with a particular work.

There are dreams we all have that remember forever though we've only had them once. I think urgent moments in our lives, the most painful, the most joyous those that stick with us. I think good fiction tries to capture those moments, and so it transcends everything else.

MG: I know it when I read it, because it makes me jealous.

WH: Do we have a responsibility as writers to write about those who have none, and thus can we give them voices, is it at all possible?

RC: The first piece of literature that actually moved me, I think I was in twelfth grade, my teacher had us read Faulkner's *As I Lay Dying.* I read that, and I thought it was a joke, you know, nobody writes about poor people, you can't get away with that. That idea was very radical to me, that you could write literature about poor people. I thought about if there were other people doing this I wanted to know. It kind of grew on me over the years that the lives of the poor are as complicated as any of the lives of all these people in the *New Yorker* stories.

VH: This may upset some, but it's a totally selfish view on my part, that I don't feel any responsibility, that you know, if people read my stuff, I don't think it would make any difference anyway.

MG: Well you can only write what you know. Flannery O'Connor said, "You can choose what you want to write about, but you can't choose what you can make live." Only thing I can make live is what I know, and those are the people that I grew up with, every hand that I shook. I don't feel any responsibility but those are my people.

I was lucky, I was the only one in my family who got out. There's not a lot of people like me who can tell that story, and it's the only one I can tell; it's the only one I know. I don't think it's a conscious choice at all.

EMW: Nobody in my family has ever read any of my books. My mother, when *East Bay Grease* came out, I presented her as how she was, and she was pissed off at first. But then she bought a hundred copies and signed them herself and mailed them to people. [audience laughs]

First time I got a story published it got to my father's house because it was during one of my homeless periods. So, he opened up the envelope and read the story, and when I came back he destroyed everything that I had in a box in the garage. He said, "How dare you!"

So responsibility to those motherfuckers, I don't think so.

My responsibility is to the truth, and I'm gonna tell it. I have paid the price, but I ain't gonna stop.

JDH: There's a book called *In Our Time* by Hemingway, it's probably the most famous book set in the place where I come from. And it may be a great book, but it pisses me off, frankly.

EMW: Haske comes over to my house all the time, says he's better than Hemingway! [audience laughs]

JDH: Well I take a personal issue with Hemingway, I don't think he understands the people where I come from, he doesn't get the people I know, he doesn't get the place that I know. He would go up there in summer and that's great, he's only fishing. I'm sure my older family and friends were up there, too, but they were cleaning his cabins. So you know it's a different world than what I see in *In Our Time*. I'll be honest, it's not so much as a moral choice, but a personal vendetta that I take with other writers sometimes.

PMF: I get nervous when asked about responsibility and art. Like it is said, maybe there is just the responsibility to ourselves. Just because I hate feeling the need to please some sort of objective, and that limits or cripples someone's creativity. There are books that are apolitical, they are funny and bizarre—and how can you write something that's devoid of politics, but informed by politics, well that's possible.

Like *Cowboy Maloney's Electric City* by Michael Bible, it's a weird little book with an unforgettable satanic gleam in its eye. Had he felt like he had a responsibility to the masses or the voiceless, then that book wouldn't have got written. Somebody's got to write about these people, somebody's got to do it. Algren did it, and he was very conscious about that.

WH: Well he said that it was the writer's job to point the finger at the judge on the bench.

PMF: Right, to be a thief, too. I heard the old idea that writers write because of some kind of personal isolation. I think that may be what draws all of us to this night world, this world of the other America that most of the readers don't see.

When I was a little kid, you know if I had grown up in a more psychologically aware place, I would've probably ended up in some kind of institution. I was not good in school, I was incredibly lazy, but I did have a great interest in weapons and fixation on pornography.

Sometimes we write about degenerates because deep down we are just like them, we are only as sick as our secrets.

RC: I just want to riff for a second on what Joe said about Hemingway. Remember that even though when I first read Faulkner, somebody writing about poor people, I realized some years later that he understood poor people but he didn't like them.

And then I found out that there are other people who understood the poor and appreciated them, like Erskin Caldwell.

WH: Faulkner wrote "The Bear," that story ends with a man driving through these woods that he used to hunt as a boy, and now it's gone, ready for the train to come in. The whole time, you're reading, you're thinking this is a hunting story, and then you get to the end and you find out that he was writing it for the people that were in the book, because, like the woods, they're gone.

Some of our greatest writers, they are very subtly political, even Caldwell. As you guys know, in contemporary fiction, you cannot be didactic in your work, is what people say. They tell you "don't write about politics."

We're taught by the intelligentsia to not get political. But look at the great works of literature and they are overtly political. Is it possible to write about politics without beating it over the reader's head? Should we be didactic?

RC: I don't think anybody reads fiction to get their political ideas.

VH: When I wrote *Fur People*, my last novel, I was being more political than I wanted to, but it was about animals and how many are murdered in each county in Florida. I wasn't trying to convince anybody, at least not consciously, but I am not sure if it is something that we can choose.

PMF: In Arizona where I live, I live in metro-Phoenix and there are politicians who want to make it illegal for undocumented people to use public bathrooms. So, this is sinister more so than segregation. It leaves someone with one option, and that's to shit their pants. But, as Gabriel García Márquez says, "If shit was as valuable as gold than poor people wouldn't be allowed to have assholes."

Here is an example of a political moment in literature that works, but in the wrong hands it could have been way over the top. *Invisible Man*, there is a scene where we find out that there is this guy who makes the paint that paints all the monuments in Washington, D.C., it's the whitest paint in the world. It is made exclusively to paint America's monuments. And the secret ingredient: one drop of black paint. Now that's transcendent and it's very political.

Or even Diego Rivera, that's an artist who takes the political and makes it transcendent. It's recently come to light, from a researcher, that where we learn to write in this country is at Iowa. Every other creative writing program is an offshoot, but it's no surprise writing got hot on the scene after World War II. Paul Angle, the director of the Iowa Writer's Workshop, got a lot of fucking money from the CIA, to make American fiction safe, and less than subversive.

Now there are a number of Iowa graduates whose work I adore, but it disturbs me that institutionally and politically we are told what not to write and what to write and we should avoid politics.

Don't write about ideas, we are told.

But, "Don't write about ideas?" What the fuck else are we going write about!?

Eric Miles Williamson

Eric Miles Williamson is the key figure in this crowd of working-class fiction writers. He played a central role in getting many of these writers published or reviewed in numerous venues. The role he has played in my own life has been similar. I met him when I was an undergraduate student in his Contemporary American Fiction course at the University of Texas-Pan American. Afterwards, he helped me become an editorial assistant at *American Book Review* and has since been an endless source of various opportunities in the literary world.

For months the two of us sat together drinking beer trying to figure out the best questions to consider for this interview. I didn't want to ask about things that he had discussed over and over again in other interviews. He refused to answer any "stock" questions about form and theory that I saw as important. It was a problem. I thought about not including him in this collection at all.

Then one day I figured that I should just record one of the regular conversations we have and then transcribe it. I thought we could have a couple of conversations and then I could assemble an interview in that manner. But in transcribing this first recorded conversation, when we are just sitting around drinking beer, we had a very literary conversation—and he ended up answering my questions about form and theory, too. Williamson's books of fiction include, *East Bay Grease* (Picador USA/St. Martin's Press, 1999), *Two-Up* (Texas Review Press, 2006), *Welcome to Oakland* (Raw Dog Screaming Press, 2009), and *14 Fictional Positions* (Raw Dog Screaming Press, 2010).

EMW: How many book reviews are as good as *American Book Review? New York Times Book Review* sucks. *Washington Times Book World* is pretty good but it's closed.

Daniel M. Mendoza (DM): New York Review of Books *is nonfiction and popular fiction.*

EMW: Yeah, but it's intellectual.

DM: Well, it's not literary.

EMW: Well, what about the *Bloomsburg Review?* And that's about it. Out of all of them I'd rather read *American Book Review*, even with all the high theory that is in there now.

DM: What do you think about that?

EMW: Whether that content is for good or for

worse, it isn't for me to say. I don't know who their readership is now.

DM: But they cover a lot of other ground, too. They make an effort to address contemporary fiction from all over the world.

EMW: And they covered working-class fiction in an entire issue. That issue was because of you. You wrote that essay about *Stray Dogs* and [Jeffrey] DiLeo thought it was wonderful. He called me up and asked me to put together an issue about my whole gang. It's exciting to see all of these things coming out. I've got *Say It Hot II*, there's *Stray Dogs*, the *American Book Review* issue on us, the *Chatahoochee Review* interview with me and [Paul] Ruffin, my keynote at NoirCon.

DM: What's next you think?

EMW: I think we need a section in the *Norton*. They've got minority writing and a lot of new women writers. But one thing they've neglected is working-class fiction.

DM: Why do you think that is?

EMW: Because it's written by guys. Mostly by white guys. The working-class has been neglected in the same way Steinbeck is falling out of the discussion,

London, Erskine Caldwell. There is a heavy upper-class, elitist preference for their own kind of fiction.

DM: There is the politically correct group, too, who wants to include a few token minority writers who aren't very original or dangerous.

EMW: What about Gilb. Dagoberto Gilb's first book wasn't very good.

DM: You're talking about the short story collection, Magic of Blood.

EMW: Yeah, he got a PEN/Hemingway for it. It should have been half as long. I was able to nominate him as a finalist for the Book Critics Circle award for his book *Gritos.* That was a good book, but his great book was *The Flowers.* He didn't get anything for that.

DM: I don't know of any other Mexican-American author who has maintained a balance between Mexican-American fiction and traditional literary fiction.

EMW: Yeah, I don't think there is any doubt that his books will last.

DM: But I wonder if they'll last because he is a Mexican or because he is a good writer within the tradition.

EMW: I think it will last because he is a good writer. His latest book shouldn't have been published and I said that in a review I wrote. But his earlier work is what will last. On the other hand, here is a guy who had a goddamn stroke; he could barely move his hands, and he still wrote a book! I don't know if I could've done that.

DM: You've written about the same amount of work, only it's much more varied.

EMW: Well, I studied more than he has. I studied English for five college degrees. I've read my ass off and learned all of the tricks. When someone with a good eye reads Gilb, they can notice that he hasn't read very much. It shows in his work.

I wish him the best, though. He hasn't had an easy life.

DM: You want to talk about Sukenick?

EMW: Sukenick helped a lot of us—he got his younger students published. He got us jobs and everything else. I teach his books still. So does Ted Pelton and a lot of others. Ron knew that if his books were going to outlive him he needed to have young people because his old friends were going to die.

I know that now, too. I knew you were a hard worker when you were in my Contemporary Fiction class, so I told you to go up to University of Houston-Victoria for *American Book Review.*

Hey, how many copies of *Anything Can Happen* do you have?

DM: Two.

EMW: Why?

DM: Well, I've never opened the other one. I'm saving it just in case something tragic happens.

EMW: Yeah, my copy's pages are all tearing out.

DM: I got two hardcopies of InForm, *too.*

EMW: Yeah? I got mine when I was a student at Colorado with Ron as my teacher. I took a course from him, an American Literature class, I think. It's a great book. He was a genius.

He humiliated us. Ron walked into class after about the fourth week and said, "Okay, half you of you in here are just writing stories that are imitating one another and the other half are just trying to impress me. So we are not having class anymore. If you write something interesting come to my office hours and I'll be there. But don't give me anything that is not interesting."

And he walked out.

DM: What did you think about that?

EMW: I felt so ashamed. I didn't see him for the rest of the semester because I didn't write anything that was interesting.

DM: That was when you were writing 14 Fictional Positions.

EMW: Yeah, that's when I was publishing a lot of those stories. But, I wasn't being myself.

DM: When do you think you started coming into your own?

EMW: It was when I got to Houston I said, "Screw this, I'm gonna write like me." That's how I ended up with *Two-Up*.

DM: And East Bay Grease *came after?*

EMW: Well, I was writing *East Bay Grease* all along as short stories. It was turned into a novel at the request of Picador.

DM: How did you sit down and write Two-Up*? Did you plot it out?*

EMW: What I did was read Dickens and Cormac McCarthy. Dickens for the plot and McCarthy for the language. I made a little chart of what happens after each page.

See, at the time, I was in this post-modern mode where there was no reason to turn the page because of the language, or for the ideas. And I figured out how these books that are heavy on plot work.

DM: How is that?

EMW: First chapter: character one meets character two and they talk about character three. Second chapter: Character three is introduced and meets with character one. Third chapter: character three meets character two and they talk about character one. And so on. Then, in the fourth chapter they all meet at the same time and they realize there is some problem they all have in common.

DM: So Two-Up *was made from looking at these general plot lines?*

EMW: I wanted to write a book that wasn't a collection of short stories or some novel that was just a bunch of post-modern gibberish that didn't have a plot.

I learned how to write a book the way you are supposed to learn: by reading fucking books!

DM: What about Welcome to Oakland*?*

EMW: *Two-Up* was all deliberate. *Welcome to Oakland* was doing, as Sukenick would say, intuit.

DM: You really believe that about Sukenick? You think he really wrote off the cuff?

EMW: Yes. He used to have a reel-to-reel recorder that he would transcribe from.

DM: Yeah, a scene like that comes out in Down and In *and* Narralogues.

EMW: Sukenick's first book was on Dial press. You know who published it? E.L. Doctorow. It was the first book and it made him famous. This was in the '60s when that kind of experimentation was all the rage, you had Robert Coover, Raymond Federman, Pynchon, and others.

They are all called post-modernists, which is really a misapplied term.

DM: How so?

EMW: Well, it's not a style of writing. It's a time period and a frame of mind. James Baldwin is a post-modernist.

DM: So Haske is a post-modernist?

EMW: No, I think the post-9/11 era is something different.

I grew up as a post-modernist, fearing the nuclear bomb every day of my life. You and Haske, and the rest of the younger generation do not fear the nuclear weapon every day. You just assume you're going to get up tomorrow. We had nuclear weapon drills when I was in elementary school. We would hide under desks and the teacher would pull the curtains so the shattering glass wouldn't fall all over us. There were fallout shelters everywhere.

And your generation doesn't protest anything at all. There are a few social protests. But there are no protests about nuclear waste dumps or biological weapons. And there are no serious protests against this war that's been going on since 2001. None!

DM: We're all cynical.

EMW: Your generation? Yeah, Mendoza, I think you're totally cynical.

You've all given up because you think the powers that be have made all the decisions and there is no way to stop them.

And no one from your generation has written anything about it.

But this too will pass in terms of literature. It's going to be a rocky twenty years. There have been periods in Western Literature where the form was sucked dry of any content. You know, after Milton there was about sixty years before Jonathon Swift came around.

DM: You think so?

EMW: How many great works can you think of between 1616 and 1720?

DM: Besides Milton? A few Shakespeare plays.

EMW: Yeah, it's totally flat. You get lame ass stuff like Richardson's *Clarissa.*

DM: I never got into the epistolary as a form.

EMW: So what made you want to become an English major, anyway.

DM: I told you before, I wanted to be a welder. The plan was get a welding certificate, go back to Hebbronville, and get a job on one of the ranches in the area. I'd make a good living that way.

EMW: Well, what the fuck happened?

DM: Initially it was the Beats. Those were the first guys that I read as a young twenty-year-old.

EMW: It happened to me too, I read Kerouac's *On the Road* when I was an undergrad. I read those kinds of books and I thought, "I could do that."

DM: See, before I read those books, I thought the idea of a writer or a poet was no longer a thing.

EMW: What do you mean?

DM: In my small town consciousness I thought people didn't do those things anymore. I thought the artist was a thing of the past. When I was talking to a community college advisor, Fred Garcia, I guess he might have had some books or something on a shelf. And we started talking about the Beats.

EMW: This is when you were with the stripper?

DM: This was a little bit after. I had been kicked out of that world, I suppose, and I was trying to get things straightened out. I was working at Pizza Hut, trying to save enough money to get a room at this tenant house in South McAllen. This nice old lady rented rooms out of this old, deteriorated house. There were about ten rooms, maybe, and a shared bathroom, shower, and kitchen. But there was a fifty-dollar deposit, and rent was only two hundred and fifty dollars.

I thought, well, I can't work at Pizza Hut all my life. I might as well get a welding certificate and move back home. So I went to the community college here and Fred Garcia, the advisor, had these books somewhere in his office.

EMW: How did you even come across books like that in Hebbronville.

DM: I didn't. The stripper I would stay with in McAllen would take me over to the bookstore and buy me books sometimes.

EMW: [laughs] How old was she?

DM: We were both in our early-twenties. I guess she thought it was a romantic kind of thing. I did, too. We were living this kind of life surrounded by drug dealers, addicts, gang members, other strippers, and then there would be these moments where we were all alone and I would talk to her about Gregory Corso's Vestal Lady on Brattle *or John Fante, or whatever I was reading at the time.*

You know, I wasn't some dude trying to pimp her out, I wasn't some pervert who hung around the strip club all night, and I wasn't a crackhead who was going to steal her shit first chance I got. She was under the false idea that I was an artist and she liked that.

EMW: So what happened with the advisor?

DM: Well after we talked for a while he says to me, "What about an English degree?" I didn't have any idea what he was talking about. He said, "You can get a degree and teach English. You can talk to people about these books you like." I didn't know that occupation, a professor, was open to people like me. I thought all professors came from a certain class.

EMW: So you did it.

DM: I said, well, I can get this degree and get a job where all I do is talk about books instead of being out in the hot sun all day. Shit, sign me up.

Anyone who has done real outdoor work—not by choice, but because they had to—knows that it sucks. There is nothing romantic about that kind of life.

Then again, I don't know. I have friends who do hard labor and they've never read Proust, they've never read Melville, Shakespeare. And I'll tell you, they are a lot happier than I am.

EMW: Yeah, no shit. They go to work, go home. Nobody fucks with them.

DM: And those that do—

EMW: Well, you settle it on the job site.

DM: That's right.

EMW: It's a good life.

William Hastings

I came across William Hastings' work when he had written several essays as the editor of the *IWW Book Review*. My mentor and friend, Eric Miles Williamson, was then a featured contributor of the *IWW* until he had written a characteristically wild piece on education in America. He was asked to resign and, because of what was accurately seen as a contradictory move toward censorship on the *IWW*'s part, Hastings resigned as well.

Hastings' work with the *IWW* was important because its readers had a valuable critic separating the few great works from the overwhelmingly bad. This is what readers need now more than ever, and you should distrust anybody who says that an insightful critic or reviewer has no place in contemporary literature. When seriously considering the amount of bad commentary in the journals and on the Internet, just the opposite is true.

At the time of the interview he was living in New Hope, Pennsylvania working as a farm hand and bookseller. When I was in Philadelphia planning to meet with some other writers, he drove up for a few days and we went back and forth on some of the questions in this interview. Ultimately, though, after several rounds of beers, the discussion would fall back on book reviewing, criticism, and the state of contemporary fiction. Between Hastings' experience as an independent bookseller and my time as an editor and reviewer at *American Book Review* and *Pleiades*, we had a lot of back and forth about what authors were worthy of more attention and who deserved a deep undisclosed place in the dustbin.

Hastings has traveled the world and has done hard labor through most of it. He's got an education, too. Taken together this is a dangerous thing to the literary establishment looking to maintain the status quo. Hastings' first book, *The Hard Way* (Tiger Bark Press, 2014), is an excellent first effort that challenges what a working-class text can actually look like. It blends memoir, criticism, and cooking into one. At the end of *The Hard Way* you are left with reflections on the state of contemporary literature and life itself.

DM: The first time I read your work was on the Industrial Worker Book Review *website, and it's a place I go back to often. You have a kind of energy in your essays that I don't really come across often enough in contemporary writers. When I read your work, other writers like D.H. Lawrence, Henry Miller, or even Hazlitt come to mind. Can you talk a little bit about your influences?*

WH: I appreciate the compliment, particularly the reference to Miller, a writer who is undoubtedly a large influence on my work, and a writer I studied closely at one of those times that happen in your life when you discover a writer at the exact moment you are supposed to be reading them. With Miller, I was living on the cheap in the Front Range Mountains outside of Boulder in a house with four roommates, three of whom worked with me bumping lifts at a ski resort. There were good drugs and cheap beer and at the time I was finishing off Hunter S. Thompson's first volume of letters, *The Proud Highway*. That was another book that was perfect for that time. In there, Thompson wrote a letter to a friend, maybe it was William Kennedy, about the books he was reading and Miller came up. I finished Thompson's book and picked up the two *Tropics*. I was pretty well read in philosophy, having studied it in high school and college, and that combination Miller has of high-flying surrealist prose and philosophy just knocked me back. Miller led me to Whitman and Whitman led me to Neruda, Neruda led me to Pessoa. This is a roundabout way of answering your question, which is to say that many things influence me, and one writer leads me to another writer. The writer I first fell for, the one that really opened my mind up was Hermann Hesse. My mother gave me *Siddhartha* when I was in the eighth grade. I devoured his books. Around that time I was also given Khalil Gibran. Both of them were early and strong influences. But I always read, and I read widely. I loved comic books and military history; I read piles of autobiographies written by Vietnam veterans. You used to see them take up whole shelves in the bookshops, all mass-markets. Tom Brown Jr.'s books I discovered as a teenager and they lead me down some great roads. High school was where I read the Beats and Hunter S. Thompson and Ken Kesey, although I didn't get into *Sometimes a Great Notion* and his wonderful magazine "Spit in the Ocean," until I was well out of college. As I said, I was a philosophy student and since my senior year of high school have read as much of that, particularly the Ancient Greeks, as I can. In college I majored in Religious Studies, which should give you an idea about another huge segment of my reading habits. My grandmother is a Lewis Carroll fanatic and so those books have been constants in my life for a long time, things I keep re-reading. My father loves Shakespeare, so there is that, too. As he should be for any writer. One of the formative reading experiences for me, one that extends its hand outward toward me today, happened while I was reading Nelson Algren's *The Man with the Golden Arm*. That summer, I was twenty-one, I worked as a lifeguard. One day I was scheduled to work at a tiny pool, a single guard one, that wasn't my regular spot. It was real overcast when I woke up, threatening rain, so I took my book with me to the pool. No one was there. After a few hours I knew no one would come to swim so I slipped into the filter room and smoked a bowl. I then went and sat on the pool deck with the book and read. I got to that point where Sparrow is in a poker game and I remember the thick gray clouds overhead, that rain almost there, and the scene read like an action movie. It was tight, white knuckle. I couldn't put the book down, I didn't want the scene to be disrupted by anything and I remember thinking that I needed to slow my reading down, that I was reading too quickly, that it was too good and there were so many things happening, and they were being told so beautifully, that I needed to slow down and really absorb them. I had always been a quick reader, but that was when I learned to slow my reading down, to see the music in the prose. Algren then, is a big influence. Hemingway was one of the writers that showed me a writer should have style. My grandfather read *Old Man and the Sea* to me when I had the chickenpox in the fifth grade and was laid up on his couch.

There are so many more, so many profound reading experiences that I could go on for days. And this is just books. The Allman Brothers Band, Miles Davis, John Coltrane, Thelonious Monk, The Black Crowes, Gov't Mule, Ray Charles, Otis Redding, Wilson Pickett, Son House, Skip James, Paul Butterfield, Woody Guthrie, Aretha Franklin, Mahalia Jackson, Blind Lemon Jefferson, the Beastie Boys and Jimi Hendrix, and more have had as much influence on my writing as any book.

I think that when we talk about influences we talk about what has shaped our intellectual and stylistic development. These things come from many places. And not all of them are books or music. What about the first time you ate hallucinogenic mushrooms or that beautiful woman you let slip away? What about Beirut or Kuwait, or those Colorado mountains? Those things shape your prose, too.

DM: All of these things have an effect on a writer's stylistic development?

WH: Style is absolutely something I have worked on, something I very consciously try to shape. It evolves, too. I hope it does, since I want it to be alive. When I listen to the Allman Brothers, any incarnation of the band, you can always tell which guitarist is soloing. Dickey Betts, Duane Allman, Warren Haynes, Jack Pearson and Derek Trucks all have very individual styles and tones. Instantly recognizable. Those styles, those tones, are very much their personality in some sense. It occurred to me early on, perhaps through listening to music as much as reading, that I needed my own style, and thus my own voice as I hear it in my head, that it is distinct and unique. Of course, that style must work in the service of what you are writing, so my style shades itself differently in essays or fiction, but those shades and tones are just part of a larger whole. We develop style by stealing tricks from other writers. Look how Hemingway used the word "and." It's a rhythmic pulse with him, one he learned from Old Testament. Take a look at W.C. Heinz's *The Professional* and you will see where Elmore Leonard learned how to pace and sculpt dialogue. Like them, like any writer, I steal from the people who I love to read and hope to absorb certain things and make them my own.

However, a writer must also have something to say. Vision. There are too many writers out there who have style and have studied so hard in all the right places that they have smooth, sellable style, but they have absolutely nothing to say, they are without vision. Style means nothing if it does not elaborate a vision.

DM: How did you get started writing?

WH: I started writing seriously, that is really pursuing the art and craft of it, when I was twenty-one. College was winding down and I knew that writing was all I wanted to do. I had to do it. It was around then that I started reading differently, reading to see how stories and novels were put together, how sentences took shape within them. I wrote and wrote, none of it good of course, and kept reading twice as much as I wrote. Devouring books of all kinds. And I kept writing and reading. There were seeds before that, things I liked to do as a kid, but those are very different from deciding to turn your life over to writing.

DM: Did you get much encouragement at that age?

WH: No one really cared, to be frank. I didn't talk much about it; I just went and did it. My life is my own and even if everyone I knew had told me not to do it, I wouldn't have listened. But I got two pieces of excellent advice from my grandfathers on my mother's side. One of them was a cartoonist for *The New Yorker* and *Playboy*, as well as a commercial artist and painter. We were talking one night about art, about making art, he knew I was writing, and he told me that in order to pursue art, any type of art, the artist has to put a set of blinders on and only chase that one thing. Doggedly. Quite a bit like what Faulkner said about a writer crawling over his dead grandmother to get the story, no? But that stuck with me in a deep way. The other grandfather wrote a few novels in the late seventies and early eighties, Wall Street thrillers that were published by William Morrow. I told him I was going to write and he told me a great story. He and his editor were at a dining club in New York. In the club there was a small room with just three tables in it, tiny for privacy and quiet. His editor waved his hand across the room and told him that all the writers in this country who could make a living solely from writing alone could fit into that room with space to spare. That was important to hear as well.

DM: I was an editorial assistant at American Book Review *for a couple of years and one of the greatest things was getting to read all of the contemporary fic-*

tion, poetry, and essays from the small presses. Often I thought I was really caught up on the work coming out of small presses, but then I would talk to another editor or writer and we'd start naming books the other person had never heard of. How does someone like you, who is well read, stay afloat amid the mass of small press publications?

WH: I work at a bookshop at night, so I have an advantage there. My job allows me to see what is coming out and weed through the piles that way. It also exposes me to what is good through recommendations from my co-workers or from customers. But, even with that advantage, there is no possible way to keep up. The ease of on-demand printing has allowed everyone and their brother to start a small press and the market is absolutely flooded. You can't read fast enough, or you can't wade through the crap to find the gems fast enough sometimes. I imagine this has always been true though. It seems like when I read writers' letters this is a common complaint. There are some good book reviews out there that cover the small press world, which I subscribe to, and the lit mags are great about providing reviews for them as well. Small Press Distribution's website is also a godsend for discovering great books. They review books on there, too.

DM: When I talk to contemporary writers, many of them will express this idea that one or another form is tired. They'll say something like, "there are too many poets and none of them are doing anything new or interesting." Do you think either fiction or poetry is a tired form, that one of them doesn't have anything too interesting going on?

WH: Even a precursory glance at half the books coming into print on any given day would leave you with the impression that fiction and poetry and nonfiction are absolutely dead. There are some awful books being published. Look at the monstrosity that is Karen Russell. But then, at the same time, there are some hellfire books out there, on major presses even, things that make me excited to be a reader. Fiction, poetry, and the essay will never tire themselves out because there will always be great writers out there who are hungry enough to make them vital. Those writers exist, many times, as a reaction to these living-dead ones.

DM: A reader can look over the American fiction of the past several decades and make the observation that there are certain things each time frame concerns itself with. The 1950s, for example, was concerned with a kind of ego-oriented fiction, whereas what followed it was the experimentation of the text—guys like Ronald Sukenick and Raymond Federman pushed this idea of the text being conscious of it being a text. Are there certain aesthetic or philosophical issues that you think a writer has to deal with today?

WH: Each writer should choose his own aesthetic and philosophical issues. While I think that the best writing is an attempt to confront how humans live, and what it means to live, how the writer does that, and from what platforms, must be decided by them, on their own terms.

DM: It would seem like this freedom to choose would create various ideologies. Some would think that is what has allowed for American literature to be in a fractured state? Do you think our fiction lacks a center? Is this a bad thing?

WH: The idea of there being a center seems to imply that there needs to be a common approach that is best, or that there should be a commonality to fiction. This I don't agree with. There should be an explosion of styles and approaches, a complete lack of a center. Anarchic. A massive variety of styles creates a large dialogue, writers reacting to other writers' approaches, communicating and commenting on them, thus pushing the form forward. The publishing system is in an odd state for sure, but that is due to a variety of factors that don't affect fiction in a philosophical sense. It affects it in a business sense, a distribution sense, but as an idea, no.

DM: I'd like to know how you write out an essay or a story. Do you begin with an outline, sketches, drafts? What's the process like?

WH: It is a little bit different each time. Some stories start with a title, or an ending that I then write toward, other times I see the beginning clear and sharp and whole. When writing fiction it is essential that the main character be fully formed in my head. I want to be able to hear them talk, see them move, see their faces, before I write. In many cases it is in the rough draft work that I discover these things. I write out the bad stuff, that is I write and get the general story down, then chuck most of that in the trash and begin again. In doing so, I have created the character in my mind and can take it from there. Hearing them speak in my head is usually the most important thing I need. Essays usually grow from a singular idea, something that I want to argue toward or pursue. For that, the idea, the thesis, is all I need and I take it from there.

I like to type out the first draft. I do that fairly quick, without too much concern for the real nuts and bolts of the piece. I just want to see the rough outline of it down on paper. That will give some shape to what I am writing, but I usually discard these. It has to feel right before I move into tightening the drafts up. If it doesn't feel right, and there is no other way to describe it, then I throw the thing out and start again. Once I have a rough draft that feels right, I will hand write that draft out onto large yellow legal pads, editing and changing and rewriting as I go. Many times I will still end up eliminating a huge chunk of the type written draft I am working from as I do this. But hand writing out the next draft slows me down, forces a good focus on the words and structure and gives me a substantially tightened draft when it is done. After the hand written draft is finished I will then go back and type that into the computer, again editing and revising as I go. When this is ready I print the draft out and read through it out loud and make the necessary edits. This helps the music of the writing. From there it is usually good to go.

DM: Do you have any specific requirements when you sit down to write? Are there things that are necessary in order for you to begin?

WH: Quiet. I like things to be quiet around me. I write with my desk facing a wall so that there are no distractions of a window view, but other than that, quiet and time are all I need. I tried writing while I drank beer or whiskey, I tried writing high, all the things you do as a writer when you are learning, but none of that produced good prose. It is always best sober, in the quiet, without anything ahead of me to stop me.

DM: You consider your writing hours to be pleasurable?

WH: Of course. That's when I am doing the thing I love the most. They are the hardest, most challenging hours, but that makes them pleasurable. What did Cendrars say, "Writing is a kind of burning?"

DM: Can I ask to what degree you think an author should concern themselves with the social and political issues of their own time?

WH: I don't see how they can't. We live in a society and are therefore tied into social and political issues, whether we like it or not. Our behavior within this society affects others in their own social and political realms. Take for example your cell phone. In order for it to work it needs coltan, a mineral, to run the microchip in it. Coltan is dug out of pits in the Congo by slave labor under brutal conditions. The phones and microchips are made in warehouses staffed by cheap, horrendously treated labor, all so that people can have an inexpensive phone to Twitter updates about their book on. Our lives are tied into others, how can we ignore that? How can writers willfully avoid taking the time to learn about, to explore and expose, these forces? It's easy to spot a writer that hasn't taken the time to understand these things. And their fiction suffers because of it. Worse, if a writer lacks a political and social push against these issues it seems to me that they can afford, literally afford, to not have politics, to just float through the middle and upper-middle class without having to confront the oppression their lifestyle imposes on others. Must be nice. Addressing these issues creates empathy, as it forces us to look inside ourselves and others. And if a writer does not have empathy, what does their fiction have? Is it worth reading? We should be taking power to task, this is what writers do—Shakespeare, Melville, Wright, Milton, Algren, Abbey, Hemingway (he wrote a book called *A Farewell to Arms* you know?), Dostoevsky, Munif, all of them have pointed the finger of judgment. If we are to honor their work with our own, we need to point and push as well.

Look at Charles Bowden's work. His books have a deep moral core to them, so much so that reading him makes you feel like so many other writers are just simply inadequate. They are inadequate because they have no moral core, no outrage. They lack vision, as I said before. Their work shows that they are fine with witnessing great atrocities, or allowing themselves to be manipulated by power, and they are neither outraged nor moved. Since they are neither outraged nor moved they write stories that are empty, stylistically good perhaps, but lacking any punch. They are little better than ad copy. You can tell many of these writers have not lived outside of the United States, outside of their language and culture, outside of their comfort zone. You can tell that many of these writers have not lived in an economic class close to, or at, the bottom. You can tell that they are not worth reading.

DM: I'm assuming, then, you would have something to say about William Gass' and John Gardner's memorable debate about the aesthetic and moral responsibilities writers have to fiction.

WH: I think the writer's aesthetic responsibility is to honor the writing gods, to do honor to the great writers that came before us by writing, and attempting to write, great work. A writer has the moral responsibility to challenge those in power, those that abuse and oppress and destroy.

DM: Do you think the function of literary fiction has changed?

WH: Fiction is meant to entertain, on one level, and to enlighten and move the soul, on another. Fiction's function is the same as it has always been and will always be, to tell a great story and tell it well and beautifully, from a place of deep thought and feeling.

DM: Besides reading and writing, what other activities are important to you?

WH: Living. I want to do it all and it is important to me to experience as much of it as I can. The things that are important to me, that I have to have in my life are: good wine, cooking, hunting—especially when it is cold and quiet and full of snow, fishing, camping, hiking high peaks and canoeing good rivers on sunny days, making love early in the morning when the heat is still trapped beneath the covers, good bourbon, laughter with old friends, soul music, blues music, country music, travel (and by travel I mean buying a one-way ticket to a country and learning the language while you live there), good open beaches, warm tropical water, deep forests, excellent books, open road and full tanks of gas, strong coffee, a beautiful and intelligent woman.

DM: What would you say is the best kind of intellectual training for a young writer?

WH: Reading. Reading in every conceivable genre. After that, travel to and live in countries other than the one they were born in, countries where they have to live outside their language and culture. They should also move around and live in a bunch of places within their own country. A whole pile of jobs is useful, too. Spending much time in bars, pool halls, boxing gyms; on farms, road crews, and in shopping malls, crime ridden ghettos and restaurant kitchens, places where their language is used by workaday people will help shape both their ears and their eyes.

DM: Is there anything that a writer can learn from other books or writers?

WH: If you can't learn anything from another writer, or other books, you shouldn't be writing.

It would be too long of an answer to discuss here what I've learned from other writers. Let me say that I hope that my work shows what I have learned and that I have made it my own to a degree.

DM: Are there books that you go back to often?

WH: Les Galloway's *Forty Fathom Bank*, F.X. Toole's *Rope Burns*, Leonard Gardner's *Fat City*, Plato *The Apology*, Walt Whitman *Leaves of Grass*, most of Shakespeare, Neruda's poems, Fernando Pessoa's poems, Ghassan Kanafani *Men in the Sun*, Jack London's *Call of the Wild* and *The Star Rover*, Franz Kafka's *The Metamorphosis*, Lewis Carroll's *Alice's Adventures in Wonderland* and *Through the Looking-Glass* and *The Hunting of the Snark*, Wilfred Thesiger's *Arabian Sands*, Richard Hugo's poetry, Joe Bolton's poetry, Catullus' poems, Bukowski's poems.

DM: Do you have any quirks?

WH: I think people that drive minivans and wear cargo shorts and go to Little League games on Saturdays are the ones with quirks. That's insane to me. In my own eyes, I'm normal.

To the minivan crowd, I probably have quirks. Hell, in their eyes I am probably totally fucked. I do what pleases me.

Stephen Gutierrez

Reading Stephen Gutierrez's latest collection of stories, *The Mexican Man in his Backyard*, is one of the greatest experiences I have had not just as a reader, but as a Mexican-American reading the work of another Mexican-American. There are no clichés in his work, and all of his metaphors are idiosyncratic constructions, which are the only kinds of metaphors any writer should ever use. His work is experimental, too, which should come as no surprise because of his early relationship with the Fiction Collective.

Though his early writing was published by the Fiction Collective, it doesn't drown itself in the influences of its founders, Ronald Sukenick and Raymond Federman—look through the catalog of current Fiction Collective 2 writers and you'll see mostly imitation. This is something else about Gutierrez; he has managed to do what few writers could: absorb all of their influences and develop something unique unto itself.

The fact is there are too few talented Mexican-American authors getting the attention they deserve. The ones that come to mind: Rolando Hinojosa-Smith, Dagoberto Gilb, Christine Granados, Juan Ochoa, Tim Z. Hernandez, Esteban Rodriguez, and of course the writer featured in this interview. But of all these only Hinojosa-Smith and Gilb have managed to garner any amount of attention. It often seems to me that critics of Mexican-American fiction focus too much on the socio-cultural aspects of the work. So what ends up getting portrayed as valuable work is merely social commentary and soap-box stomping.

Gutierrez, as an example, is not only one of the more talented writers of contemporary Mexican-American fiction but of contemporary American fiction as a whole. There are very few writers who have made an honest attempt to move away from the formal experiments of the post-modernists. Gutierrez does this well, blending biography with fiction and theory in ways Ronald Sukenick's *Narralogues* envisioned for the future of the experimental novel.

When Mexican-American literature decides to take itself seriously as an art form that values aesthetics over the soap-box, Gutierrez will find his rightful place among its greats. More importantly, however, when the gatekeepers of American fiction cease to view writers by the color of their skin and instead value them for their aesthetic and didactic accomplishment, Gutierrez will be valued as a great American writer. Gutierrez's works include *Elements* (Fiction Collective, 1996), *Live From Fresno y Los* (Bear Star Press, 2010), and *The Mexican Man in His Backyard* (Roan Press, 2014).

DM: Do you think novelists have the power to influence the culture in America?

Stephen Gutierrez (SG): Yes, I do. I think if somebody possesses the right voice that is an appealing echo of our own collective interior voice and says what it wants to be said, but isn't articulated usually because of fear or general societal restraint or tradetion that can happen. That prophetic utterance can be taken in and effect a shift in consciousness—in how we think, act and do. It would take a remarkable writer to do this, and maybe the traditional form of the novel would be an inadequate vessel for that voice.

DM: How so?

SG: The idea would be banging against the walls of that chamber as within an empty room, needing a fresh way of announcing itself. The voice we're talking about is prophetic, again, new and fresh. I don't think the standard way of structuring a novel would woo it to its greatest heights. It would at least semi-reinvent the novel while attaining its power.

DM: Is this why some writers choose literary fiction?

SG: I can only answer personally. Everybody does it for her or his own reasons, none bad, really, if the act doesn't hurt anybody. I write literary fiction because it feels good to do so, literally, the mind is engaged, the imagination activated, the deepest part of my brain's pleasure center, that to do with language is stimulated. It satisfies me, makes me happy, very, very happy, the act itself. I suppose this positive outflow of my best energies can't help but be a boon to the general malaise in the air due to the usual culprits—TV, the baseness of our consumer culture however manifested in abased language. If one spark of mine inspires another in a fellow writer or eager reader that is reason enough to go on. To upend boredom and complacency with challenging feelings is a fine thing to accomplish. To excite. To thrill. To move. Hell, yes. Reasons enough. I mean to truly do those things, not to spoon feed the mind with predictable drivel as in too many movies. To charge language while it's still possible is probably the greatest reason to keep on. It's one of the mightiest tools to remind us we're alive. So much conspires to say we're not; literary fiction, at its best, gives hope because it taps into a deeper sense of life than non-literary fiction, that's for sure, or most movies, again, and much else that passes as art. I'm not saying I'm an artist. I'm saying I write literary fiction because it's important to buck the trends that are shallow and strive for depth, which needs no justification. The hope in it comes from the closeness we may feel to human experience that isn't our own, but that feels just as real. We aren't so alone.

People should write literary fiction to cure lonelyness. I think its influence on our wider culture is minimal. Its influence on literary culture is moderate to strong. We're still waiting for the great bridge people, those writers who can say something important and fresh and appeal widely, without compromise.

DM: This kind of closeness is what you want readers get out of your fiction.

SG: I hope that they experience being alive as another person in another time and place and learn (again) that we're all pretty much the same facing the same shit, sometimes nobly, sometimes ignobly, but that a great pull towards decency is the one that should prevail. If they come away with a sense that my spirit breathed some life into the English language and feel that difficult (for me) feat is a sign of human commonality, being a desperation we all share to one extent or another—to breathe life into the words we use to tell our stories, even orally; if they come away with having known life on the page, yes, I'm happy, because every time we share life and/or accept the life spirit from another that is a great stride toward human understanding and acceptance. I hope they connect with me, sensing me behind the curtain, and know that I love them.

Otherwise, I wouldn't write.

DM: Are obligations of morals or aesthetics something you ever think about when writing?

SG: The writer just tries to make the best thing he can with the materials he has created pounding away at the keyboard for that magical word or phrase around which a composition can truly grow—around his strongest possible utterance, literary utterance. An aesthetic plan will emerge from that discovery, and, yes, then the writer is bound by the contract he himself has begun to lay out in the incipient form or shape that the work is taking. But, no, the writer has no obligation to any aesthetic creed considered outside the necessity of the actual piece that engages him or her at the time. None. No obligation, either, to morals, particularly as our sense of morally correct and incorrect differs widely from person to person and background to background. The question, as I read it, implies some standard of morals we can refer to. Maybe not. At any rate, the writer is not a lawgiver or even a law reminder, though to be one is a great thing, a law reminder. But that is not his primary duty. His only task is to make it as well as he can, the thing itself, and interest the reader. Personally, I think his obligation is to render human experience accurately in as striking a composition as he can, and that striking does not mean merely eccentric or anything easy, but sound, aesthetically, structurally, sententially sound. But that's only me. God bless.

DM: What do you think you are like compared to the central voice/character in The Mexican Man in His Backyard?

SG: A lot like him, I think, particularly as many of the essays—hybrid pieces, really—in the book are deeply autobiographical with little embellishment. I am amazed and aghast at life, its dark beauty. I also possess a sense of humor at its bitterest moments—I think that is in there, a certain merry despair.

DM: In this autobiographical position that you take in The Mexican Man in His Backyard, *and some older pieces as well, there is a similarity with post-modern writers like Ronald Sukenick and Raymond Federman.*

Sukenick once said that the motivation to take an autobiographical approach to fiction was to "tell some truth beyond your personal vision and beyond literature itself." Would you say you are working around the same theory?

SG: Certainly the truth must be beyond your immediate understanding or experience to encompass everybody's and transcend the merely personal, which is usually tied up with unflattering ego, however hard we try to portray ourselves as ultimate victims, which is what I read again and again. It must get at something big, even if that large thing is really basic and simple in the end—whatever that truth is, it should be one that leaves the autobiographical figure in awe, not a truth that he deigned to share with you as sole possessor and jealous discoverer. And to get beyond literature? Why, yes. Literature sucks. Imaginative writing is pretty awesome, though, if it's skilled enough and knows where it comes from.

DM: Some of the pieces in this collection, like "The World Came Crashing Down on My Wife" and "La Muerte Hace Tortillas" can be read as highly personal, but they also reflect a social dimension.

SG: "The World Came Crashing Down on My Wife" includes mention of that fierce battle of a previous generation about the hiring of minorities at universities. The notion of this being contested seems a bit quaint now, but the real feeling of minority sub-standard-ness was in the air then, a very smelly odor, posed against the whiff of general white mediocrity (I don't mean to be offensive but just to make a larger point), of pervasive averageness. I think the story does a service even to our current social landscape by making alive this pattern. Does it still exist? I don't know, rightly, but if it does then more power to it, the story. "La Muerte Hace Tortillas" is a relevant piece of social history, I would say, busting open the notion (again "notion," I don't have a better word here) of hegemonic "Latino" thought or attitudes as expressed in the different takes on the Vietnam War in the Mexican-American community then, and even in the attitude towards *cholismo* as expressed in the mother's horrified response to her oldest son flirting with it. Well, it's just decent social history like the "The World," I would say, and that's reason enough to make it socially relevant now. I put quotation marks around "Latino" by the way because I am uncomfortable with the term. I don't really consider myself a Latino, it seems fraudulent in defining who I am. I am a highly assimilated Mexican-American working-class guy. Many members of my generation are frauds in calling themselves "Latinos." But I'm a fraud in other ways so it all evens out.

Finally, I did not consciously intend to make these pieces socially relevant. I just wrote them as well as I could, digging into memory and using my imagination to explore a certain theme in each. The writer is more beholden to theme than anything else.

DM: A lot of Mexican-American writers use the traditional Realist model for their work. Why do you think the Realist model is still so dominant for minority fiction writers, or even for most fiction writers?

SG: It's easy, it's convenient, it's what we read in our very formative years and it makes sense, theoretically. There is a nice way to tell a story, with a beginning, a middle, and an end. However you change the order, it's still going to have those hills and valleys that make up story land. The model at hand, the traditional landscape/form looks pretty good, eh? But my mind is messy. That is probably the single most important reason why I stray.

DM: Other writers whose work can be seen as ex-

perimental assert the idea that the mode of fiction should change with the times, they express a dissatisfaction with the idea that many fiction writers still work with a nineteenth century narrative model. Would you agree that the model of fiction should change in an effort to become more relevant to the culture?

SG: I would agree that we need something new to be heard. I think many writers are strong enough to compel attention in the old narrative model, and that is all to their credit. But I also think the writing that might speak to the culture most deeply is yet to be invented, or always being invented to reflect the era. Of course the model should be changing, shifting, growing. Look where rock 'n' roll has come since the '50s. And we're still using a nineteenth century form? I think one should be at least aware of how tentatively the walls are set up in the old house, and not be afraid to demolish them.

DM: Can you talk about your relationship with the Fiction Collective?

SG: I know some of the folks associated with the press, both the editors and staff as well as Fiction Collective 2 writers, not well, but comfortably enough; a smart, savvy, talented bunch, no doubt. And shaking things up for the right reasons, not to be rabble-rousers, but because they're honestly bored and annoyed by much that passes for "fine writing" for good reason. It's mediocre. It's stale. It's a small step away from pre-packaged commercial fiction no matter how loud the plaudits of the critics who bestow important awards on it. Some of it, mind you. Some of it. There are serious, intelligent talents running this alternative press that is honest in its mission to publish what the big houses or mainstream presses won't touch but what has literary value. I know them because I won a contest they no longer sponsor and had my first book published by them. I might send them a purposefully retro, anti-literary, anti-experimental experiment in plainspoken storytelling soon. Test their limits.

DM: Elements, *your first collection, was with Fiction Collective.*

SG: *Elements* was my first collection. It is a reworking of my MFA thesis done for Cornell. The long essay, "Sad Days in Haytown," came separately. I just kept reworking the stories until they felt right, published them in magazines high and low, literary and funky, I mean, and won the Nilon Award for Minority Fiction sponsored by FC2 at the time. Grand prize was publication, plus a thousand dollars.

DM: Can you talk more about the process of revision?

SG: It varies story by story. Sometimes it is extensive, entailing a whole new vision or great chunks of new writing that a fresh scene demanded, a tweaking of a weak sentence inspired. I go at it in constant rereads of the story that reveal weaknesses where I thought lay strength and rework the story until it is all sounding right, is all of a piece. Sometimes the revision is minimal, no more than cleaning up what is there. I don't really consider that revision, but editing, fine-tuning, an entirely different thing. Revision is replacing parts in the motor, hell, dropping in a new motor because the old one sucked—no roar, no purr, no danger to it. I put on dirty coveralls and scoot under the story in my study, wrench in hand. I know nothing about cars, by the way. Only how to change a tire. Revision is not about changing a tire. That is, again, editing. Get dirty.

DM: Did you get much encouragement early on?

SG: Kind of. Sort of. I was always good at "creative writing" in elementary school and middle school and got encouragement from teachers who recognized my biggest academic strength, writing and an imagination to propel it. This is going to sound extremely hokey, but I won a school-wide writing contest in the eighth grade on the theme of "Who Am I?" and pocketed twenty-five dollars in first place prize money and felt pretty damn good about it. Later, in high school, I didn't do much writing of any kind except bad, academic writing I was being semi-decently trained in but couldn't get, really. My mind was so messy and confused then, hell had broken out at home. But when I went to college my mom encouraged me to take a creative writing class. "You're good at it! That's what the teachers have been telling me since you were little." Of course, when I made my intentions known that I really wanted to write and do nothing else, the typical response followed: "You WHAT? How are you going to support yourself?"

DM: Can you talk about your upbringing?

SG: I was raised in City of Commerce right outside the borders of East L.A., but not in it, the barrio. I came of age in a working-class neighborhood in the '60s and '70s, born in 1959 and was pretty happy, miserably, until things got bad at home with the onset of my father's early-onset Alzheimer's in the early seventies, around 1973. Then other stuff happened to make me even more miserable and I've never really escaped the pain of those years—as I write, my chest tightens. I fled to a state college up north after high school, wanted to be a writer, started to write. But to speak of my upbringing more generally: hardworking father, laboring for the railroad, neurotic, bright mother who loved to read, a sister I got along with, an older brother whose desperate, tragic life was related to the hereditary illness in the family (he died at forty-four of early-onset Alzheimer's), me the youngest, bright, confused, tormented in adolescence, truly unhappy. Working-class Mexican-American, a big step away from the barrio next door, which I still knew of from hearsay and cousins who lived there and cholos I got to know here and there, good guys, bad guys, crazy fuckers, bright dudes, dull ones, you know, the usual assortment of people anywhere. We spoke English at home, that's my first language, it surprises me when people even ask. I heard a lot of Spanglish growing up, a lot of Spanish around me, too, which I understand fairly well, but don't speak. I grew up a Southern California dude a la Chicano. My mother had a great reverence for learning, for school. My father worked hard for us until he couldn't, wrench in hand, trainman's kerchief around his neck, oil-stained.

DM: What did your parents expect you to be?

SG: Well, way back when before my father got sick they expected me to be a success of some kind, a professional. When he got sick and the whole household fell apart, including, of course, his mind, rendering him incapable of expecting anything from me, my mother also ceased worrying or thinking about my future. It was all about survival, daily survival—economic, emotional, psychological survival. But we had a term for guys like me back then, "college material." It applied to bright girls, too. I was bright. It was expected that I wouldn't work in one of the factories around the neighborhood but would succeed in some professional field of my choice, using my brains, not my hands to make a living. The thought of using one's hands to earn one's bread was associated with brute labor back then, not with any skilled trade that would be respected then, as now.

Michael Gills

I met Michael Gills at NoirCon in Philadelphia where he was to take part in the Stray Dogs discussion panel, which is also included in this collection. His editors from Raw Dog Screaming Press gave us a ride back to his hotel lobby because I had to pick up some batteries for the tape recorder. Afterwards the four of us—Gills, his editors, and I—walked over to a bar that me along with JD Smith, Joe Haske, and Eric Miles Williamson had shut down the night before.

Gills proved to be the opposite of everything Williamson had observed of him—earlier that week Williamson had said the Gills may prove too self-involved for a good interview. When I told him about what Williamson had said, he returned jokingly, "Well, it's not like Eric has ever been accused of hyperbole!" We sat around with a few drinks during the interview. Gills ordered food for the table and a whiskey for himself. His questions were insightful, he had made sure that his answers were thorough and was always willing to elaborate on any aspect.

Gills' work is southern in a poetic kind of way, whereas Ron Cooper's—another southern writer—is more philosophical. Readers will notice this mostly in the language, which is often heavy on the play of sense imagery and illustrative metaphor. What you remember most from a Gills' story is not what this or that person said, or the overall narrative, but an image or a scent. For example, in the story he contributed to the *Stray Dogs* anthology, "27 Trap," one remembers the scent of oranges that came off the character Dayna Barges' yellow dress, or in "Whiskey For Breakfast," which ran on the *IWW* site, one remembers springtime in Arkansas.

If there is any writer in this collection that can render the working-class beautiful it is likely to be Gills. *Why I Lie* (University of Nevada Press, 2002) his first collection, achieves this kind of working-class beauty. It's a complex text because its language—full of density, metaphor, and southern dialect—is so much more unique than many of the southern writers publishing work today. Gills has published other works since *Why I Lie*, including *Go Love* (Raw Dog Screaming Press, 2011) and *White Indians* (Guide Dog Books, 2013).

DM: Do you think people live too long?

Michael Gills (MG): Did you ever read *Gulliver's Travels*?

DM: Sure.

MG: There are some kind of people in there that

never die and they are some of the bitchiest, mean spirited people in the whole book. All they wanna do is die. I don't know. You consider in terms of the species. The average age of the human species when we first started out, when they first started moving across the continent, people died at about thirty-six years old. So that is when all these discoveries were being made during the great migration, these people were teenagers. That explains why teenagers are in a hurry to get out and live, it's still there, it's a part of our species.

And my daughter's sixteen.

Today people are living longer than they should.

DM: What do you think about the academic community's contribution to literary fiction—here I'm talking about working-class fiction?

MG: Have they contributed? The reason I've gotten into the academy is because I can't make it as a writer. I don't know anybody that can. I know one person that can make a living as a writer, and that's Julianna Baggot. But, she's crossed a threshold and I don't really want to read what she's writing anymore. Even she after her third book she was having to teach to make a living. Teaching gives me time to write.

I get up every morning and write from four-thirty to eight-thirty five days a week, I couldn't do that, I couldn't support a family any other way. So the academy, I guess, that's what they do.

DM: Four-thirty in the morning is how you start your writing? Can you talk more about this?

MG: I am usually finishing up as the sun is coming up, and it's hard to fuck up a day like that, when you've already done your writing before daylight.

DM: Do you always work on something specific?

MG: I always have a project, I've got things on a bulletin board. Right now I'm finishing a first draft of a novel. I go forward, I never go back. When I finish it, then I type it out. I'll revise it and then I'll start the next project.

DM: I can't remember how I came across this, but I heard you start off longhand, then typewriter, then computer?

MG: Yeah, and I'll mark edits as I go along. When I have a final manuscript then I type it out on the computer. The University of North Carolina's got the special collections, and they took all those drafts of my work for research.

DM: How do you feel about that?

MG: Good, I think it's pretty cool. Plus I was able to get rid of all my suitcases full of manuscripts that were in our basement. You know who gave me the idea, Eric (Williamson)! He said the University of Houston or somewhere said they were interested in his papers and so I found a place where they pay you and let students research it.

DM: I heard about that, I think it might have been Texas Tech who was interested in his papers. Tell me about the new novel. Does that start with an idea or an outline, how does the process play out for you?

MG: I've got outlines mapped out on my wall where I write, right now. I've got twelve of them, enough to last me about the rest my life. So I finish one book and go on to the other. *Go Love*, my first novel, it's part of a quartet. I wrote the second book first, and now I'm writing the first book. But, I'm finding out there are problems with doing that. I didn't know I was going to write a book that preceded *Go Love*. Then I've got *White Indians*, there are two parts to that. I've got a group of short stories that I just finished, I'm going to be marketing two books at once. It's mapped out from here on out for me. Not that something else will happen, as it is I got plenty of work from here on.

DM: You think you'll get them all done?

MG: You have to write yourself into shape, like working out. Right now I've been working five nights a week three hours a day. I'm at the point where I can make moves I want to make that I couldn't do before when I was just starting out. Plus, I'm able to coordinate what I'm thinking with what I put on the page, and that takes time.

DM: You ever get anxious when you don't write?

MG: I don't get anxious I get out of shape.

DM: In the lobby you said, you had a hard time distinguishing between the nonfiction and fiction. How important is the ego?

MG: When I get working, and I'm consistent, I'm not really caring about what anyone else thinks about me, I'm just caring about the work. Now that's separate from trying to market the work, you know when you get rejected and you're feeling like shit. There was this editor. He rejected a piece of mine one time, I was at the point where I really needed to get something published. He wrote my rejection out on a piece of vellum with a manual typewriter: "Dear Michael Gills, I cannot accept...." So I took the rejection, flipped it over and I stapled a ten dollar bill to it, and I said "Dear Bob, here is ten dollars that you can either shove up your ass or go buy a drink with, I don't really care, thanks a lot, Michael." He wrote, "I accept your implicit invitation, dipshit, I used the ten bucks," and he carbon copied Fred Chappell, William Morrison, Jim Whitehead, Jim Clark, all of my mentors. What that says about ego, I don't know. It still hurts to get rejected.

You ever been hunting, when you're in the hunt, when you get on the trail with something, you're not really thinking about ego, you're thinking about what's in front of you, what you're doing.

DM: Does that translate into the idea of audience? Do you think much about readers?

MG: I think if I'm caught up in what I'm doing, and it's electric for me, then it will be like that for my intended audience. I don't want somebody to like me. You know that's a big word now, I'm so sick of that word "like." I want to move you. I want to engage you, that's what I want.

DM: How hard was it to achieve that level of writing when you first started out?

MG: When I teach prose, I teach five elements: point of view, structure, language and tone, conflict and character. I was taught that by William Harrison. Bill Harrison, he's a brilliant writing teacher and he taught me that. I was really good at point of view and voice, conflict, tone, language, I had no problem with. I grew up with some really far out people, so character I had no problem with. When it came to structure, I sucked. Bill actually came up to me and said, "Michael, this is really good stuff, but you ain't worth a shit at structure, you got to get better." So what I did was structuring and structuring, so it was back in North Carolina where I had all these graphs of my work structured out, laid out. So for me learning the importance of structure.

DM: Like line graphs, timelines?

MG: I end up with, something like, in Faulkner's house, he didn't use paper, he actually wrote things out on the wall. But I got a whole wall of novels laid out. Do the characters and everything else end up happening the way it's structured, no, but I got a map, since I got a map I can be spontaneous. If I didn't have a plan there would be chaos.

DM: You have an education in literature and creative writing.

MG: I was the first person in my family to go to college and I went to college as an athlete. I was a football player at Arkansas. I started out as a journalist, but I made a D in Grammar for Journalists.

Here I was from a family where no one went to college. And I said I want to be an English major, my dad said, "What! What the fuck is an English major?" I said well, we read literature. He turned to me and said, "What the fuck is that?!"

I was this sophomore at the University of Arkansas when I won a graduate-level prize in writing. I ended up winning that prize three more times. It gave me hope, it inspired me, it let me know that I wouldn't end up in prison.

DM: Does your family read your books.

MG: No. Never. Not at all.

DM: Some critics think that every writer tries to find himself through the characters he creates. Do you agree?

MG: When asked where Emma Bovary came from, who she was modeled on exactly, Flaubert said, "C'est mois"...me. In that sense, I don't make characters up. They come sort of full blown—maybe I hear their voice first. Not even sure I create them, more like net them, gig them, noodle them from a hollow log.

DM: Is character the first thing that comes to you when you begin working on a story?

MG: Usually it's something I remember: a picture of a zebra that when I look at it I remember there was this all deaf football squad that used to practice across the street from me, with deaf cheerleaders who'd grunt and thrust their hips, so I'd know they were doing "Satisfied..." Then the whole shebang rolls out and I end up with the *New Madrid* story "The House Across From the Deaf School."

DM: Your work is a lot different than most of the writers in this collection. People can call it working-class fiction. I can accept that. But your form is much more unique. Why I Lie, *for example, is a complex work of highly poetic prose and metaphor and density. Can you talk about metaphor for a moment?*

MG: Sure, the rule about metaphor is that it has to function as what it is first. A tree stump has to be a tree stump before Parker can drive his tractor around it. A tattoo is a tattoo, and a wooden leg is a wooden leg. Then, after the thing is fully grounded, you can blow the goddamn roof off with it. But it has to be itself first.

DM: Do you think fiction should teach lessons of any kind?

MG: Chekhov answered that one, as did Kafka and Faulkner in his speech accepting the Noble Prize. A book should lift up the reader, like an ax that splits us open and lets out the ice water inside.

George Williams

George Williams has published one novel and three short story collections. His novel *Degenerate* (Texas Review Press, 2010), a road novel of sorts, relied on experiments with punctuation and unconventional description to carry the narrative. His three short story collections, *Gardens of Earthly Delight* (Raw Dog Screaming Press, 2011), *Valley of Happiness* (Raw Dog Screaming Press, 2015) and *inferno* (Down & Out Books, 2015), were a departure from his novel's syntactical descriptions but preserved the distant voice of the narrator, which has become a kind of signature to Williams' aesthetic. In these three collections there is an inherent desire to rewrite the traditional allegories of our culture in order to make light of the issues that plague our culture now and, to paraphrase JD Smith, another writer in this collection: the social conditions of globalization and technology.

Williams' work in all of the collections is probably most reminiscent of Donald Barthelme. This should come as no surprise seeing as how Williams, along with Smith and Eric Miles Williamson studied with Barthelme at the University of Houston. Like Barthelme, Williams finds humor in our contemporary social environments, but it cannot be separated from a kind of terror that resonates under every situation. It is this dichotomy that he is constantly trying to illustrate in his works, and it is one that brings to mind older writers like Gogol.

Though Williams' work in *Degenerate* may appear to differ radically from his short story collections, this desire to come to some kind of solution is apparent. The solution, in all of his works, however, is a very inept and human one.

Like Williams' work, the answers given during this interview were complex. On first look, they do not give much away, at least not directly. This characteristic, however, is similar to the narrative and even speakers in his works. Williams says at one point in the interview: "If I'm doing my job, the inference to be drawn is always more interesting than the action." This, his own observation, can be applied to his answers during this interview.

Williams can come across as different than many of the writers in this collection; his work isn't specifically concerned with the working-class. What he is concerned with is coming to terms with how our culture works now and illustrating the issues and responses various people take in light of these new workings. For that, Williams' work is one worth engaging.

DM: I think it was Philip Roth who posited this idea that the writer of contemporary fiction has a much harder time getting at the truth today as com-

pared to other times in the past—say in Dickens' time. Would you agree?

George Williams (GW): Getting at the truth? No. Getting it to an audience, yes. In Charles Dickens' time, the novel had a near monopoly on leisure time spent at home. Imagine working as a software engineer, a social worker, or a chemist. After a long day, where do you turn for entertainment? A smart TV or a novel? There are readers out there, to be sure. Even if you include genres like science fiction, international thrillers and fantasy, whose readers are mostly men, eighty percent of novel readers are women. If they quit reading novels, the genre truly is finished, though writers have written about, and satirized, the death of the novel for at least the last three generations. In Barthleme's "The Explanation," a story published almost fifty years ago, in which nothing is explained, Q asks A, "Is the novel dead? A: Oh, yes. Very much so." A few lines later Q asks, "Is the bicycle dead?" During the half-century in which its death has been reported again and again, some of the best novels have been published. *The Loser. Blood Meridian. Light Years.* Most recently, Elena Ferrante's Neapolitan novels.

DM: How does artistic responsibility fit in?

GW: Irresponsibility is the higher calling. Leave responsibility to crossing guards and bus drivers for the minimum-security prisons called public schools.

DM: You mentioned Barthelme. How has his work or other post-modern writers been influential on your work?

GW: "Post-modern" is a tricky, untrustworthy term. Barthelme dismissed the category because he was unwillingly put on the same "football team" as writers like Robert Coover, whose fiction is as boring as Barthelme's is brilliant.

DM: In a recent article in the American Book Review, *Charles Harris said something about the split that still exists between Realism and experimental fiction. He seems to believe that the projects of guys like Barthleme, Coover, and Fiction Collective are being continued by contemporary experimental writers like Lance Olsen, Matthew Kirkpatrick, Matthew Roberson, and FC2 while the Realist novel is still working with a tired nineteenth century model. How do you feel about this observation?*

GW: All fiction is experimental. If it amuses, engages, delights, then it isn't an abject failure. Among my favorites is Thomas Bernhard. *The Loser*, *Woodcutters*, *Extinction*. Comic novels filled with dread and finally pathos, in which nothing much happens but much, too much, is remembered by misanthropic narrators who are savagely funny.

DM: Wouldn't you say that your work brings together realism and those experiments that the writers of the '70s and '80s were working on? Anyone who reads Degenerate, *for example, wouldn't exactly say it is a work of traditional realism or high experimentalism.*

GW: Every story, or novel, writes its own rules as it's written. I had none of those considerations in mind. Among the many flaws of the novel: why is he telling the story?

DM: Let's talk about style for a minute. The most obvious stylistic element of your work is your use of markers: road signs, billboards, etc. You're able to use this effectively as a way to drive the narrative forward. For example, in Degenerate *mostly every section uses this element. In your shorter collections it is not used as much, but it is apparent. How did this come about?*

GW: *Degenerate* is a road trip novel, so it seemed fitting. I spent more than a decade driving back and forth from Savannah to Houston three or four times a year to visit my daughter, so all that freeway time had to have an effect. I was impressed by how many travelers I saw at rest stops and truck stops who looked like they'd packed up everything they owned and were heading somewhere to start over or trying to leave a personal catastrophe behind. Until recently, no people on earth uprooted and re-rooted themselves more times than Americans. The downturn of 2008 changed that, but I'd hazard it will change back. A chapter in de Toqueville's *Democracy in America,* "Why Americans are so Restless in the Midst of their Prosperity," helps explain why we are traditionally such a deracinated people. That his explanation still obtains almost two hundred years later is remarkable. Also, one of the ways I start a story is to take a few inchoate characters and move them across a landscape and see what happens.

DM: Talk about how you chose the artwork on the covers of Gardens of Earthly Delight *and* The Valley of Happiness. *What's the relationship to the fiction?*

GW: A panel of Bosch's triptych I had in mind for decades. The cover of *The Valley of Happiness* is Bruegel the Elder's *Magpie on the Gallows.* At first glance it looks like a condemned woman is being shoved by two men to the gallows, where a magpie sits like an omen. A closer look: the three are dancing.

DM: Do you know what your earliest memory is?

GW: Neuroscience tells us the best way to preserve a memory is not to recall it. Every time you summon a memory, it's revised, combined and recombined with others, so whatever I think is my earliest memory is probably a collage of impressions. Do I think growing up on Signal Mountain, Tennessee, gave a two-year-old a love and a fear of heights? At the end of the Cumberland trail look down into the Tennessee River Gorge and tell me that isn't what a nineteenth century writer saw in the Alps: the sublime. Beauty tinged with terror. So my earliest memory, or sensation, is one of falling off Signal Mountain.

DM: What has been the most enjoyable story you've written so far?

GW: "Wabash," "California Poppy," and "Lagoon" were the most amusing to write. I can't claim to know which stories if any readers will find enjoyable.

DM: How do you feel about the popularity of what has been called literary memoir in this country?

GW: Puzzled. I have little interest in reading them or in writing one. In his fifties and again in his sixties, Nabokov published *Speak, Memory.* But writers scarcely into their third or fourth decade are publishing memoirs. Their first books. What next? Lynn Nesbit says literary fiction, if it's not dead already, is dying, "an endangered species ...there are more writers than readers. It's because of the memoir. Everybody thinks they have a story." It's not surprising a few of the most successful have turned out to be lies, i.e., novels sold as memoirs. Nabokov was already ahead of that game. *Speak, Memory* is as much fiction as fact. A butterfly he was chasing reappears forty years later in America. Why are they so popular? Because we are overwhelmed by fiction everywhere we turn? Television news, hundreds of cable channels, the Internet? Because of reality TV? The influence of social media? I don't know.

I was amused but not surprised to read that the more time you spend on social media, the more isolated, lonely, anxious and depressed you are likely to be. Jaron Lanier calls it "digital Maoism." He also believes corporations have co-opted the idea of friendship and sold it back to consumers. I asked a friend whose judgment I trust to create a Facebook account and tell me what he thought. He was reluctant, but he did, and wrote a wonderful one-line impression: "a howling chamber of loneliness." Now the co-founder of Facebook has made it his mission to make sure no one on the globe is disconnected from his anti-social "social utility," so he wants to make the entire planet a howling chamber of loneliness. The phrase "social utility" ought to bring to mind the worst abuses of language of the last century—think *radiant future* — but so far as I can see it doesn't. Megalomaniacal foolishness meets digital totalitarianism. Perhaps memoirs are a way to slow down and take refuge from this mayhem, the latest version of what Bellow and others called "the moronic inferno." The good news: I hear millennials and younger are fleeing Facebook.

On to another circle of social media hell.

DM: What was the last novel to be the single most important contribution to American literature?

GW: I can't know that, nor can anyone else. Only politicians and genocidal maniacs truly believe they're smarter than the future. No cradle rocking above an abyss for them.

DM: No author crosses your mind?

GW: I'd hazard James Salter's *Light Years* and *All That Is.* To publish a masterpiece at eighty-seven. Most fiction writers are finished by forty and never write one great book, let alone three or four.

DM: Who have been your biggest literary influences?

GW: That's really a question about the reading life. Shakespeare, Chaucer, Homer, Milton. Dante, Rabelais, Swift. Charles Dickens. The first day of eighth grade English, the teacher, a small, waspish woman name Mrs. Green, said to the class, "Come in, sit down, and shut up." She read to us the first chapter of *Great Expectations.* I was born into a bookish family, but that was not a book, it was a narcotic. That year we read Homer, Shakespeare, Keats. No Young Adult literature, which didn't yet exist, thank God. Mrs. Green would have not wasted our time on it. For my age I was fairly well read when I was a freshman at Sewanee, but the first day of class the professor Douglas Paschall arrived with no book in hand and wrote on the blackboard in beautiful cursive every passage to be discussed. I had a lot of catching up to do. I read very few contemporary writers until I was in my early thirties. Thomas Pynchon, whose *V* and *Gravity's Rainbow* I read when I was far too young. John Kennedy Toole, Walker Percy, Robert Heinlein. Then I discovered writers like Donald Barthelme, John Hawkes, Padgett Powell, and Joy Williams, the best short story writer going. Again, I had a lot of catching up to do.

DM: What is the biggest lie we tell ourselves?

GW: All my characters lie, white lies, self-serving lies, outright lies. A thousand shades of truth and in the shades more shadows of half-truth and the endless capacity for self-deception. Poor, forked, credulous creatures who want the truth they already know they cannot bear.

DM: Do you think you are writing fiction that is relevant to the social context that we live in?

GW: One hundred years from now. That's the biggest lie I tell myself.

Patrick Michael Finn

Eric Miles Williamson was the first person to give me both copies of Patrick Michael Finn's books: the short story collection *From the Darkness Right Under Our Feet* (Black Lawrence Press, 2011) and the novella *A Martyr for Suzy Kosasovich* (Cleveland State University, 2008). Re-reading both works numerous times, I am constantly surprised by their achievement. The novella is a tough form for any writer to work with. I can think of only two or three classics that actually succeed at it; they are Voltaire's *Candide*, Kafka's *The Metamorphosis*, and Bellow's *Seize the Day.* One other contemporary work that I believe do the others justice is Tom Williams' *The Mimic's Own Voice* (Main Street Rag, 2011). It is Finn's short story collection, however, that is the favorite of mine. In it we get to see the author's capabilities in a larger sense. Finn is at once a creator of vivid character, complex plot lines, conflicting themes, and most of all idiosyncratic metaphor and symbol—it is these last two things that I believe elevate working-class fiction to a much higher place than other genres of contemporary literary fiction.

"Shitty Sheila" is the third story in Finn's collection, and it does a great job of illustrating what he's up to in his fiction. Sheila is a stripper in Joliet, Illinois. Her initial goal was to get to Chicago where a couple of girls from back home had a job for her. Sheila never makes it; instead, she goes from stripping at the Pink Pony to posing for cheap adult magazines, and finally, trying to turn tricks in hotel rooms. Along the way, the reader meets others as downtrodden as Sheila. She takes the reader in and out of Joliet's horrible depths, together witnessing every character's demise, and finally, turning to the final pages, we read of Sheila:

> On the day the doctor came to tell Sheila she was dying of lung cancer the skies outside her window were the same ugly color they had been when she first came to Joliet, friendless and lost and wandering for three days in the rain.
>
> "Cancer," she said.
>
> "Yes."

"Shitty Sheila" and the other stories in Finn's work present an awkward question. What, besides witnesssing an artful display of tragedy, can the reader take from *From the Darkness Right Under Our Feet*? Of "true art" John Gardner wrote that it was "too complex to reflect the party line," and that "it tears down our heroes and heart-warming convictions, violates canons of politeness and humane compromise." In Finn's work you will not find generic protagonists, you will not be lead in one way or another toward that generic goal: "optimistic closure" and you won't come across characters trimmed close, too perfect to believe. Instead, you will encounter characters, like Shitty Sheila, who are absolute products of the harsh environment the author has created for them. Some of the central characters will have you cringe at their deformities or ethics, but none will make you think their actions are insincere to their beliefs.

Another interview with the *International Workers of the World-Book Review* posited the question of content, why does he take as his subject matter such depressing and unflattering characters? Finn's response: "Who wants to read about happy people doing happy things? I don't. I want to read about people who are in deep goddamned trouble. And that can take place in many different fictional landscapes." Finn's work succeeds because of its aesthetic rigor and its refusal to follow the "politeness and humane compromise" that a reader often encounters in realist fiction. Finn's two works *From the Darkness Right Under Our Feet* and *A Martyr for Suzy Kosasovich* are acute examples of not just working-class realism but high realism, and for that reason they are admirable fictions for a young writer.

When it comes to the short story—which is the go-to form for most MFA creative writers—no one comes close to the literary achievement of *From the Darkness Right Under Our Feet.* There are few writers today who will spend close to a decade revising a work with the level of energy Finn has. American literature can only benefit from any other work Finn will publish in the future.

DM: It used to be a common supposition that writers who shared the same kind of content, or writers who were often grouped together by critics, had a lot of communication with each other—I'm thinking of the "lost generation" as the most famous. Do you communicate often with other writers you see similarities with—guys like Eric Miles Williamson, Ron Cooper, Michael Gills?

Patrick Michael Finn (PMF): Yes, I talk to Eric quite often, and it's great to hear his growl on the other end of the line. He can talk about anything. Music, philosophy. Literature both great and horrid. And Donald Ray Pollock and I stay in touch. When I was on Facebook, Ron, as well as his wonderful, hilarious spouse Sandra. I dropped off Facebook back in May. Man, I miss Ron and Sandra. I've gotta get back in touch with those folks. Steve Davenport as well. Fantastic poet. I communicate the most with Adrian Van Young, the brilliant short story writer, novelist, and critic who lives in New Orleans and teaches at Tulane. Goddamn, his collection *The Man Who Noticed Everything* amazed me. Simply amazed me. I'm also in touch with William Hastings, a power-house fiction writer and memoirist. His book *The Hard Way*, which I was honored to blurb, is unforgettable. Locally, I hang out with Joshua Rathkamp, another fantastic poet. William Boyle, author of *Gravesend*, is a fantastic individual. Brother from another mother. And then there's Gonzalo Baeza, whose *La Ciudad de los Hoteles Vacíos* is being translated "from the Spanish" as they say, by Joseph Haske, author of the terrific *North Dixie Highway*. What unifies this big group of writers I'm in contact with is a phenomenal taste for the kind of books I love. They tell me what to read next. I'm their loyal disciple. Sometimes we have similar backgrounds, sometimes we don't. But at the end of the day, I wouldn't say I'm exclusively in contact with those who share similar tendencies on the page in our writing.

DM: You're a big reader of contemporary fiction, then?

PMF: George Saunders says, "We don't really read books. We read authors," and I agree with that sentiment. I may not be the most Catholic reader in the world, but when I become completely and totally obsessed with a book, I'll devour, line by line, like I said, everything from that author's factory. So right now, yes, I'm reading a lot of contemporary fiction, as much of what's been published in English by Bolano has been so within the last ten years. But I think the REAL question you're asking is do I read many more recently-published books, and that answer is no. But I used to read the *Best American Short Stories* every fall up until a couple years ago. I got bored with the content, sad to say. And I don't read many book reviews. No, wait, that's not true. *The Millions, The Rumpus.* Sometimes I look at those online, but I've rarely seen a review for something contemporary that makes me want to jump up and buy it.

DM: Literary fiction is not the most glamorous high art form out there today. So what worth is there in writing in this type of form?

PMF: For me, the worth is right in the work. Figuring problems out on the page, problems in the story, making (hopefully) fascinating characters, landscapes, and scenes with my own imagination. Trying new things. Orwell said something about inner-demons compelling us to keep writing, and I think that's true in my case. I have obsessions, terrors, fixations—death, sex, violence, the explosive passing of every second between the past and the future—that I'm trying to make sense of and give shape to in the form of the story and the novel. You're right in that literary fiction may not be as glamorous as—well, shit, what kind of high art still has any glamour in this country? Symphonies are shutting down left and right. I suppose the glamour for any artist is almost entirely interior. The wonders of the imagination at its most surprising and spectacular, which is a private joy, but breathtaking nonetheless. Until very recently, I used to believe that a work of art wasn't complete until it was beheld by its intended viewer, but I think that's crap now. I don't know why I changed my mind about that. Maybe because clinging to that belief charges the pressure to have a bigger audience, which means writing to please others. I don't care about pleasing anyone. In the end, I truly don't. I feel like I'm at my most creative when I don't have an intended audience in mind. The only subject or individual I'm obligated to please is the work laid out before me—those characters and landscapes. I woke up at 3:30 this morning because I felt an urgency to move a particular character through her house without waking her father, a scene that may be the opening moment of the novel I've been working on for the last five years, and there's no glamor, no money, no fame or anything that pulled me out of bed to get that scene right. Only writing the scene itself. Or I should say rewriting it for roughly the tenth time.

DM: Were you ever tempted to pursue any other art?

PMF: No. Fiction has always required so much of my focus and attention that I've only and always had eyes—and time—for fiction and fiction alone. Anything else, any other pursuit of another medium, would be fraudulent dabbling that would invariably lead to a pile of shit.

DM: Dorothy Parker used to write poetry because she said it helped her prose be more precise.

PMF: I started as a poet, I think, and of course, as usual, a horrible one. But I love to read poetry, and I often read poetry before I write fiction, and in reading it I'm looking not only for the art of precision, as Parker did, but for that special way of seeing and articulating the world in only the way a great poet can. I strive for a poetic sensibility in many—but not all—moments in my fiction, when time and chronology aren't as important as the metaphysical transformations, reversals, images, and metaphors I work to weave into my stories. The qualities that divide artful fiction from less-than-artful fiction, I suppose.

DM: Can you talk more about the writing process?

PMF: Sometimes I get an image or a character's name, or a visualized gesture of some sort, or a line of dialogue, and sometimes I get a few words in my head that would make a great title, and I start scribbling. The first steps are always written with pen and pencil, on notecards, notebooks, scraps of anything within reach. Everything I write then takes on its own process of how I eventually complete—or abandon—whatever it is those initial cells of an idea compelled me to write. I don't think I've ever used the same organized process to complete a story more than once. Once a story eventually starts to let me know what it's about,

I'll outline, and very roughly, how to get to the end. Or I'll sketch endings. Then along the way I kick out lots of drafts. False starts, wrong turns. I'll polish ten, fifteen pages, find I've written myself into an impossible corner, then ditch them. My story "Shitty Sheila," for instance, is forty-two pages typed, but it took two hundred twenty-four pages of drafting, sketching, rewriting, and outlining to eventually pass the finish line.

DM: Is the initial organization of a story just as random?

PMF: I always let it develop over time. Sometimes for a very, very long time. Years. I never, ever know what a story will become or how it will end when I start it. I started the story "For the Sake of His Sorrowful Passion" in October of 1998 during my first semester of graduate school at the University of Arizona. It was first called "Cairo by Midnight" and was uniformly (and rightfully) slaughtered in workshop. A month later, the revised version was called "Bastard Dan Returns from the Long Current." Again, the workshop took it out to the courtyard, tied it to a post, and lined up in firing squad formation to put it out of its misery. I remember the impetus for wanting so badly to get it right: Stuart Dybek's "Visions of Budhardin," which employs a parallel present-action and past-action structure of narrative momentum. I wanted to replicate the same structure.

Ten years later, I finally understood how the story needed to be written, what it required, how the characters needed to come to life. But it took that decade and the hundreds of books I'd read in that time and the thousands of pages I'd written to learn what that story needed in order to function. And even then, ten years later, I ended up working on the story exclusively for six months, hundreds of pages. The images of the canal and the boy's ridiculous boat kept haunting me during that decade. I knew all along I'd go back to it someday.

Weird, the Union Pacific freight just rolled through about five miles south of me, the horn going, just like the last scene in that story. It feels like a pat on the back.

DM: How about the writing schedule?

PMF: I don't have the luxury of a strict schedule, so I carve it out whenever and wherever I can. I'm a loving husband and a father of a seven-year-old son. My family comes first, no matter what. Honestly, that wasn't always the case. For the first few years of my son's life, I was hell bent on writing every day, chained to the notion that if I didn't write every day, then I wasn't a real writer. You know, that indoctrination you get from your writing teachers. But shit, man. I would have made an excellent candidate for a death cult. If those teachers had told me to stick needles in my balls in order to write, I would have. But you start to notice how many prolific writers leave many unhappy loved ones in the wake of their relentless production, and I don't want to abandon those loving faces who greet me with hugs and kisses every time I walk in the door. So I no longer write every day, or sometimes every week. This past summer, I barely wrote a word. My wife was very ill, hospitalized several times. A brush with death. Writing wasn't possible. And it shouldn't have been. Not in those circumstances. I have no weekly or daily quotas for how many pages I need to write. I do think young writers benefit from that daily regimen, but I'm forty-one now, I've completed two books, I feel like I know what I'm doing, and my sense of self and grounding and wholeness comes from the time I spend with my family. Add to that a five-five community college teaching load, which I can't help but put a great deal of energy into, and so I don't watch much television or see many movies, though of course I want to. I simply want to read and write more than that. If I'm writing, I have to read. There have been periods when I wrote and put reading on the backburner, and the writing was consistently uninspired, pedestrian, and flatly unimaginative.

DM: Are your writing hours pleasurable for you?

PMF: Like any serious endeavor worth pursuing, writing hours can sometimes be pleasurable, but they're also stressful and frustrating at times. Stories and novels don't come with instructions. But I wouldn't say I hate writing, the way I hear so many other writers say they hate it. Those hours ease something inside me, even the stressful days. I take poet Stephen Dobyn's advice when I sit down to the page: "Lower your standards." I actually write that on top of the page before I start. It frees you from the obligation to be perfect, since perfection isn't possible anyway. Even if I know what I'm writing is going to get tossed or change vastly—and change is inevitable—I can be a pretty happy camper when I'm scribbling away. Trying. What matters is trying. I've given up a couple times for fairly long periods of time, like a year and a half, and I was miserable. I lacked will, lacked confidence. And this was after my second book came out. I fell into a suckhole of despair because I couldn't figure out how to write the novel I wanted to write. I'd been trucking along on it for two years, then wham, it had a heart attack or a stroke and fell over and died. I think I was burned out, honestly. I was thirty-seven, and I'd never taken a break since I was twenty-one, when writing became a full-time job. That's sixteen years without stopping.

DM: What about when you are not writing, do you think you are a very observational kind of person, do you often look for material to include in your work?

PMF: I think I'm curious and observational, bordering on voyeuristic. I love eavesdropping. I wish

I had the jack to buy a shitload of surveillance equipment to listen in to what's going on across the street or down the block. If the three of us go for a walk at night and happen to pass an open window, I want to crawl up and stare inside. What are you hiding in there? What are you watching? Looking at dirty pictures, you old cad? I'm always looking into people's cars. If I see a tower of smoke even fifteen miles away, I drive to see the fire. When three squad cars go racing down Baseline Road, I follow them. I'm known to hang out in bus stations and truck stops on occasion, especially in the middle of the night, down on I-10 halfway between here and Tucson. I like to watch the world most of us don't see. But I do go looking for material in the form of honest-to-Christ bookish online library database research, old newspapers, books. Nonfiction. I'm writing about a long-haul semi driver now, have been for the last five years, so I need to know everything about that, equipment, schedules and long-haul drivers are simply too busy to answer my trifling questions in order to sit in the comfort of middle-class writing to make their labor serve my art.

DM: You have some great titles in your work—I'm thinking of really emotional titles like "For the Sake of His Sorrowful Passion." Do the titles come to you as you are writing?

PMF: Sometimes titles come to me as I'm writing,

and sometimes I have a title in my head for years before I know the first thing to do with it. I carried "Smokestack Polka" around in my head for three years before I wrote that story. I had to finally do it justice before it cheaped out on me and turned into some twisted euphemism for fucking down in the basement of my filthy, filthy mind. But "For the Sake of His Sorrowful Passion" comes from a Roman Catholic prayer/chant I grew up hearing (my family is Irish-Italian Catholic) called the Chaplet of Divine Mercy, and that line is sort of the chorus, over and over and over, and if you listen to it, you can probably find it on YouTube, you'll hear how much the dismally-sad tone matches that of the story's. I think the greatest education in title writing I got was devouring Barry Hannah—especially *Bats Out of Hell.* Where in the fuck else in the universe can you find a title like, "Hey, Have You Got a Cig, the Time, the News, My Face?" Or "Upstairs, Mona Bayed for Dong." Those titles are poems themselves, I don't give a fuck what anybody says. They charge on with sabers drawn, galloping in that dirty gray of the Lost Cause, coming to chop my head off and leave me in the mud, slick with the blood of the Confederate dead.

DM: Some readers can look at your fiction and see a kind of social dimension to it. I've noticed that class struggle and poverty are familiar topics in your work.

PMF: Now perhaps more than ever before, given

the U.S. has the third-highest poverty rate in the industrialized world, right behind Turkey and Mexico. I work every day on the front lines of impoverished America. My students come from the Barrio, the Rez, the houses and apartments their parents have to rent because they lost their jobs and homes, houses and apartments from which they'll likely as well be evicted when their owners lose their jobs. Happened to my family in the early '90s, and that was a little recession compared to this one. People are fucking struggling. Many of my students work two jobs on top of taking a full load of classes, which, even at a community college, are far too expensive. I thought I was put upon working at that bowling alley. Some young women here turn to topless dancing and webcam porn for quick money. That rips their souls out, based on my experience of how that changes them. So yes, to a large degree, I do consider myself—at the risk of sounding soap-boxy—an intentionally political writer. I didn't always, since, again, many of those writing profs often told me to never consciously write about politics. But every word someone writes, whether the writer knows it or not, is a political choice, of course, informed by institutions that have raised and continue to inform the writer. Christ almighty, do I sound like a raging Stalinist or what? But goddamn, I live in the landscape of tyrannical Mexican-haters that is Metro Phoenix, where politicians want to make public restrooms off-limits to folks without papers, for starters. Which, in its own special Maricopa County way, is more sinister than segregation because that leaves one with only the option to shit in his pants. So we'll have to see where the tide eventually turns on that one. I'll keep you posted. Until then, if you even want to come out for a visit, you, sir, better have your docs on you, because the Maricopa County Mounties will pull you over to make sure you're legal.

DM: That's happened a few times driving only as far as North Texas.

PMF: I suspect there are quite a few writers whose version of staying informed is an hour of "All Things Considered" on the way home from their comfy gigs at the U. I don't hear them yelling about Obama's NSA spying program, for instance. Lots of complicit, well-meaning white liberals out there are churning out books, as far as I can see.

DM: Do you think the short story medium asks for a higher degree of control and technique than a novel or novella?

PMF: I'm not sure shorter forms require a higher degree of control and technique than do longer forms, but *different* degrees of control and technique. It's a completely different ballgame writing a novel, so I've found. What Frank O'Connor calls "The Character of Time" that often differentiates stories from novels (though I'm not in complete agreement with his rigid definition of the difference between the two), requires a great degree of sophistication in how it's technically executed in a novel, as does the large cast of characters we see in novels like Donald Ray Pollock's *The Devil All the Time*. To keep those overlapping plotlines, those series of recognitions and reversals, with such an ensemble requires a control I've not experienced in any short story I've ever read or written.

DM: Have you learned a lot from reading different kinds of fiction?

PMF: I've learned how to control language, how to determine what needs to be known and what can be left out in the final draft. I've learned what parts of real life to focus on, while keeping the boring parts out, as Hitchcock advised. Books have showed me the nuances of dialogue, how to keep it sounding real without sounding as boring as real speech. Pace. Control as well as meaningful excess, which is never as excessive as it seems. And I've also learned what to avoid. Like characters who spend too much time alone, navel-gazing about their cheap, first-world insecurities. Or characters who watch a lot of television. Or characters who reach disposable epiphanies.

DM: You're still pretty early in your career, and you've already put out notable work. Do you think a writer's talent fades, as he/she gets older?

PMF: Shit howdy, I hope not! I'm getting older by the second. White whiskers. Low testosterone. Have to give myself a shot of T in the thigh once a week with a spike that hurts like Christ almighty murder.

I honestly think most writers I admire get exceptionally better with age. They often get less precious with their language because the clock is ticking and they have stories to tell. I see a lot of urgency with age. Urgency and less of a desire to howl, to please, to show off. Of course, there are always exceptions. But I have high hopes that my best is yet to come. Even if, in the end, it never sees the light of day.

Juan Ochoa

Eric Miles Williamson prefers the term Red-Neck Noir, and in an important interview with Paul Ruffin and Ron Cooper that term appears again and again. Labels, what to call this group of writers when I first began this project was a task, especially for me, someone who would rather not give these kinds of things so much importance.

But does accepting that term mean we disqualify minority writers like Juan Ochoa, Stephen Gutierrez, and Rolando Hinojosa-Smith? Or what are we to make of writers like Richard Burgin, whose characters are not really redneck or working-class at all? The term Williamson used in another interview for the French literary magazine *Transfuge* was "meta-fiction." That seems like an appropriate term with the exception that meta-fiction does not allude to the working-class.

I am talking about all of these things in Juan Ochoa's interview because of all the writers it seems that he is the one who provoked the issue of identity in my own experience. His novel *Mariguano* (Texas Review Press, 2013) shares many of the tropes of the working-class novels that other writers gathered here have written. Things like poverty, notions of success, the American Dream, and excess are things that Ochoa's characters struggle with as they develop throughout the narrative. But what sets Ochoa's work apart is the notion of politics and race, especially along the Texas-Mexican border.

Ochoa treads a very delicate path in this novel in regard to this last observation. It is very easy to fall into cliché as writers like Gary Soto and Sandra Cisneros have done, and it is very easy to be labeled more a Latino author than an American author, as writers like Rigoberto Gonzalez have done. In fact, I can think of only one writer who has made a very successful career in both spheres—appreciated by Latino critics and American critics—that is Dagoberto Gilb.

From this perspective, Ochoa's work becomes very difficult to talk about. It is difficult to separate the aesthetics of *Mariguano* from its politics. Now, politics is something that many of the writers in this interview collection care about but for some reason it is much more apparent in Ochoa's work. Is it because he is a Mexican-American writing in one of the most Mexican parts of the country, a part of the country that is rampant with Mexican influence? I am not sure.

How does Ochoa feel about politics? You can expect the same aggressive voice in his work to appear in this interview. He doesn't hold back about what he believes literature can and cannot do, or what the contemporary writer's goals are in this country. He has a particular opinion about the role of the Mexican-

American writer in this country. Though it isn't one that I can say I totally agree with, it is one that I continually think about.

DM: Your novel Mariguano *can be read as a work of fiction, but it also addresses a lot of political and social realities that are very pressing for this country. Do you think novelists have the power to influence the culture in America? And is that something that should be a primary aim of literary writers in this country?*

Juan Ochoa (JO): I think of what Rizal and Achebe were able to do in the Philippines and Africa, and it's clear that the novel is a powerful tool for social upheaval. I think the challenge for most mainstream American authors is finding what to challenge from all the social issues that are currently plaguing our nation. As a Mexican born in America, living on the border, it might be a little easier for me to write from the angle of someone experiencing occupation, certainly not on the level of the aforementioned but nonetheless in tune with the political alienation and the limited upward mobility as well as the disconnect with the ruling class. So I try to hone my writing skills to that effect, as an instrument of social change because my environment demands it. And I'm not sure anyone can sit down to write a novel without at least a little of that notion because otherwise why would we tell that particular story in that particular way? Even if the writer doesn't sit down with the primary aim of influencing some aspect of culture, if the work is done right, the influence is inevitable.

DM: You think the novel is an important tool for change?

JO: In many aspects, novels can do a lot more toward telling the truth than non-fiction. With non-fiction, stories have to be documented or at least corroborated. There are legal issues with libel and defamation that writers have to worry about. A missed date could discredit an entire work. With fiction, a writer can tell a story as real as it gets without the logistical hang-ups of non-fiction. With a novel, a writer has the opportunity to be the guy pulling the strings, unfettered by norms or sanctions other than the critic's pen, which most writers tend to ignore anyway unless the critique is good. When you keep in mind that every war starts and ends at the tip of a pen, then it is easy to comprehend and be humbled by the power of a novel.

DM: There aren't many Mexican-American writers studied in academia by cultural theorists, post-modern theorists, and literary theorists. A response to that kind of observation is there are so many other Western European writers in the canon than Mexican-American, or even Latino writers.

Is the attention of the academic community—to be

studied by critical theorists—important to you? Would it be of any use to readers of your work?

JO: To have the attention of the academic community is important to me because this community gives access to the people who can actually do something like start a social movement, the young, the students. I would like for my work and the work of many other Mexican-American writers to be given much more attention by the academic community because the work merits attention. I think we are doing things with language and story telling that is forever going to change the American novel. In the future, as we see demographics change and minorities become majorities, it's the hyphenated American novelist that is going to bridge the communication gap and open roads for inclusion. Readers of my work could benefit from critical theorists because any instruction and discussion is better than none, and the academic community can build an audience as well as a platform for this type of writing that might otherwise go unnoticed by other communities. But in the end, the attention from my people and community and their acknowledgment that I got the story right is more important than having professors deem me worthy of the canon.

DM: So you think the attention Mexican-American writers get will change as the community gets larger, and perhaps more educated, in this country?

JO: Oh most definitely things will change, but I'm not sure in which direction. Our community may lag behind in educational opportunities but not in smarts. The question is will we ever be given a platform that is equal to white or African-American authors? For the Mexican-American writer to be taken seriously, America has to recognize that it is still practicing slavery. It has to recognize that the legal system is a for profit machine that breaks up Mexican families with complete and total impunity. African-American authors have a platform because many of the injustices they write about happened "in the past" and we as a nation have "moved on" from those dark chapters. But for Latino writers to be taken seriously, society has to acknowledge the fact that after African-American people were released from the bondage of the American agricultural fields, it was Mexicans who took their place and are still there to this day, with the boss using deportation as the whip and the federal government providing the man hunters should anyone try to run away. I think it is really hard for people to recognize the horrors that our immigration policy has created that include government sanctioned concentration camps in the form of immigration detention centers. It's hard to recognize that our policies promote indentured servitude, sex trafficking, child labor, etc. especially when everyone is yelling "U.S.A-U.S.A.-U.S.A!" I don't think it is a question of being taken seriously. I think the issues we as writers bring to the table are too serious for what the academic world can handle. Remember, most of our professors were white, and they didn't like it when the conversation turned to oppression of minorities and were always quick to point out that that was then.

DM: It's important for Mexican-American writers to discuss certain political or social issues in their work.

JO: Why write if these issues aren't going to be addressed? I think Mexican-American authors need to break away from the "I'm a poor Mexican, please love me anyway" story and get down to the business of freeing our people. We have a drug war to stop. Our kids are being taken from us and put in foster care because of a draconian marijuana prohibition policy. Walls are literally going up to keep people who look like me out of this country. I can't be the only Mexican in America that sees something wrong with all of this. I'm confident that sooner or later Chicanos will remember that we built the pyramids, we played among the stars, and that when Cortez hit the beach, he encountered the most advanced civilization on earth, and that this recollection will cause for more of us to grow a pair and stop hiding behind hyphens and come out as Mexicans swinging from bell to bell.

DM: You spoke earlier about "truth," can you talk more about that in regard to the novel?

JO: The truth. Every writer knows that sooner or later it's going to come down to him/her or the story, and the story is always going to win. So the novelist goes into the fight knowing full well the outcome, but if he/she approaches the work honestly and remains steadfast to the truth no matter how unpleasant or unflattering for the author, the fight can be exited with dignity despite the defeat. Anyone who was raised like I was knows that beating up the big kid on the block is not the road to respect—it's usually just the road to the ER. The only road to respect, self-respect and the respect of your peers is just showing up for the fight, especially when you know you are going to lose.

DM: Do you believe that a writer's best work is informed by the experiences in their life?

JO: Anthony Quinn said in *Zorba the Great*: "Any man who has a life worthy of writing about has no time to write." I was both blessed and cursed to experience what I did. I was blessed in the sense that I got material to write about on the surface, but below that, the blessing came in the fact that I was able to make sense out of a situation and tell about it. The curse is obviously all these experiences were very traumatic and oftentimes painful to remember. Whose experiences aren't? We all have to cope with our realities, and I think that is what writing is all about for most of us. I believe in the "levels of narration" theory where everything plays an influence. I don't think anyone can sit down and write a piece of fiction that is completely detached from them personally with success because it is obviously not real. I can't write about hugs and kisses from mommy and daddy with any credibility because I never got any. The same applies to writing about my parents burning me with cigarettes because that never happened either and if I did try to write that, it would be an insult to all those who have lived this trauma. I think the line between autobiographical truth and fiction is drawn by the story. Sometimes the writer has to break away from the life story or the events that shaped that life and allow the story to be born and eventually surpass the reality. The autobiographical truth is one thing, but for the writer, reality and being able to mold a story that best exposes that reality is the true art.

DM: What aspect of writing was the hardest for you to develop and how did you get through it?

JO: The hardest thing for me was trying to write like a writer. I kept wanting to be like Burroughs or Márquez, but then there's Fuentes and Allende, Borges as well as Fitzgerald and Hemingway and on and on. I kept wanting to develop a style comparable to these guys, but of course this is impossible because I am not these guys. Finally, a friend and mentor told me that everyone seemed to like the way I told a story when we were sitting around a case of beer. And this made me remember that I come from a long line of great storytellers. My grandparents, parents, aunts, uncles, friends, neighbors all were unofficial historians for their families, handing down oral histories oftentimes as our only inheritance. So when I finally figured out to just go with what I was raised to do, the writing became much easier and satisfying.

DM: Do you have any other projects that you are working on?

JO: I'm working on everything and nothing at all. I have started a screenplay, which is currently going through a major overhaul in my head. I'm working on the sequel to *Mariguano, El Penal.* I'm trying my hand at editing. But like Hawthorne said, "No man can consider his life his own when he has undertaken the challenge of raising children." Work, family, and the inevitable procrastination that I get when I start to wrestle with an idea for a story has me in a constant take-off stage at the moment. I'll hit my stride pretty soon because I can't stand myself when I don't produce, but for right now, I'm still sparring.

DM: Can you talk about the influences of your work? I'm interested in knowing how you feel about Rolando Hinojosa-Smith, Gloria Anzaldua, and others from South Texas.

JO: A lot of why I set my novel where I did and

used the real names of the towns and direct references to prominent figures in Rio Grande Valley history was because Hinojosa-Smith was not afforded the same luxury. In his works about the Valley, the towns were changed creating a Faulkner-like Valley, one that could be but that was obviously not real. Anzaldua was credited with taking a more radical approach, at least radical for the time, which I liked and helped open some doors to expressions that were useful to me. I got a lot of influence from Beat writers like Burroughs and Kerouac who wrote about Mexico. I think it was Carver, but I could be wrong, who had a story set in the Valley, only he called it Bonnie and Clyde country. All these helped me. But a lot of the help came in the sense of teaching me what not to do. I know that might sound pretentious, but I don't think a lot of these guys got the Valley. Anzaldua wrote about the Valley through her rearview mirror. Hinojosa-Smith wrote about the Valley he hoped it could be. The Beats and other Anglo writers saw the Valley and Mexico from the outside looking in, and I'm not saying that their observations were wrong or that mine are better. I'm just saying that I was looking for something else when my pen was scratching out *Mariguano.*

DM: And the canonical writers?

JO: Poe, Irving, Hawthorne. These guys were able to create pieces of work that are still relevant, and I think this happens because of what these guys chose to write about. Irving and Hawthorne's observations on society, politics and laws and how these are manipulated can be seen today with the way some groups have been able to have a negative yet overriding influence on simple issues like gay marriage, global warming, political alienation—we're still cheering for the new boss who is the same as the old boss. And of course Poe taught us that the worst horrors are found in our own head. I think that every writer has a little of Young Goodman Brown in him/her. I think we sit down and write because, like the protagonist in this story, we've seen things and we'll never be the same for the experience. And it is maddening, which might make us all false narrators, like in Poe's work. But of course the influence cannot be limited to traditional western literature, even though it is a good foundation. I firmly believe that the writer who produces more than he/she reads is practicing a hollow trade.

DM: In Mariguano, *characters like the Old Man become individuals that the reader is invested in—they're humanized. This is a different story than what we would hear if the Old Man was only talked about on the evening news.*

JO: I make no secret about my work being autobiographical. The Old Man character was based on my own father, but that was only the beginning. Over the course of developing this character, elements of other people I had met who did the same line of work my father did began to emerge in the Old Man. The character became many people, but I always wanted to maintain the elements that made my father extraordinary amongst his peers. I think the trick when developing a character is to stay true to whatever element made the character appealing to the writer in the first place. If a writer can do that and still have the character function and move and evolve with the story as it unwinds, readers will invest in that character. The reader can identify and even care about the character no matter how despicable they may seem on the surface because, if it's done right, the reader can tell that this character is real, even if it's made up of several different people. As long as the elements that were employed to develop the character are real and the effort is honest—with no lean toward bias or personal prejudice from the writer—the character can come to life and the reader will care because it is just that, life.

Ron Cooper

When I think of philosophical fiction, like most other people, the work of Albert Camus comes to mind. His novels *The Stranger* and *The Plague* outline what the existential philosophy meant for him—though, like all great writers, he would have never admitted to such an interpretation of his work. Nonetheless, when readers think of seminal existential works, *The Stranger* and its lead character Meursault come to mind. All this despite the fact that Nietzsche's *Thus Spoke Zarathustra* and Kierkegaard's *Either/Or* probably do a more creative job at blending philosophy and fiction.

With all the works coming out of the presses today, it is easy—and perhaps lazy to categorize each and every writer, to relegate them to a singular position in the literary world. Amongst the small presses, writers are either aligned to the publishing houses that print their work or an aesthetic movement. I think of the Crab Orchard poets whose work is an embarrassingly honest attempt at the likes of WH Auden's and Wallace Stevens' more accessible work, or the FC2 writers whose work though impressive at times will never come out of the shadow of the original Fiction

Collective—but that is not a bad place to take in the shade.

To come across an array of contemporary philosophical fiction writers may not be hard, I would presume. But Ron Cooper is the only one I can think of, or rather, he is the only good one I can think of, since Camus. Now, of course, Cooper would never admit to writing philosophical fiction. But after a fifth or sixth reading of his novels, *Hume's Fork* (Bancroft Press, 2007) and *Purple Jesus* (Bancroft Press, 2010), this is what I always think about.

Cooper is in a curious position. He isn't writing from his east coast or west coast university office in the ivory tower, no, he is writing in a working-class Florida home. Or maybe he writes in his office at the community college where he teaches.

Is Cooper doing what his other working-class contemporaries are doing only with a more direct philosophical message? Is he trying to set forth some kind of philosophical ethos to the working-class gang I have grouped him into? These were the kinds of questions I was interested in asking him.

Work is an integral part of Cooper's second novel, *Purple Jesus.* A couple of things struck me as important while interviewing Cooper. The first was the subject of labor in his books. He had said something in the interview that I was sure many of the other writers could feel a sentiment for. To paraphrase, he had said that with the very idea of labor for the working-class came a feeling of struggle. There is the struggle with the world, to at least get by in it. The other thing is the idea that work, real work, is tough, and nobody that has ever done it has ever said they enjoyed it.

That last observation he made is important because it is often overlooked from a critical standpoint. As I write this I am well aware that working-class fiction is on its way to becoming a kind of vogue genre. In an obvious way we can see writers like Daniel Woodrell gaining attention on a national level, and I would even say reality TV shows like *Duck Dynasty* and *Gold Rush* further illustrate the culture's interest in working-class lives.

For the most part, I think those who have received national attention have a way of romanticizing the working-class, especially the "labor" involved in the daily lives of this class. This romanticization of the working-class—to make it into a commodity— is to render it harmless. To read the working-class authors gathered in Hastings's *Stray Dogs Anthology*, and to read *Purple Jesus* especially, the reader sees that Cooper's observation of work is the only meaningful one.

DM: Are you superstitious about anything?

Ron Cooper (RC): No, although I tend to be a creature of habit. I usually write in the same place, and I like to keep my handwritten notes for whatever project I'm working on in little pocket-sized journals. If I don't have that particular journal for that particular work-in-progress with me at all times, I feel separated from what I'm working on and will resist making notes onto some other medium.

DM: How's a day of writing begin for you anyway?

RC: When I wrote my first novel, *Hume's Fork*, I had a stack of detailed notes from thinking about it for many years. I finally decided that I would no longer be that guy who carries on about the book he's writing until his friends start to avoid him. I wrote the first draft in about three months over one summer, mostly in the morning and then editing at night. *Purple Jesus* was done mostly at night in a small room connected to our garage over a year's time. That experience took a real toll on me, and I went into a period of depression that, while I don't think was caused by writing, certainly was exacerbated by all those agonizing hours spent alone and being hard on myself. I also felt a good deal of guilt about the time spent away from my family in what is—let's face it—a supremely selfish enterprise. For my third novel, *Gospel of the Twin,* I took a much more casual approach and wrote at varying times and for shorter stretches. This was quite good for my psyche. My college has generously granted me a sabbatical for the spring of 2015, so for my next novel I'll be able to write in the morning when no one else is at home and avoid that guilt altogether.

DM: Do you listen to music or drink much when you write?

RC: No, I generally like quiet when I write. I don't drink *as* I'm writing, but I suspect I drink more during those times that I write compared to the weeks that I take a break from writing. Regardless of what anyone says to the contrary, writing is hard as hell, and it can take a real psychological toll. I think few people are cut out for serious writing and even they tend to develop emotional scars from it.

DM: Tell me about your life growing up. What made you want to become a writer?

RC: I grew up in the swampy woods of Low-country South Carolina. My parents come from small-time tobacco farmers, and most of our neighbors were involved in some sort of farming. I learned to love the outdoors—I hunted and fished incessantly until well into adulthood—but I also understood that, for most folks I knew, nature was something they struggled against. They constantly worried about whether there'd be enough rain this week and whether their crop would make enough to pay off the bank loan and turn a profit. Those who weren't farmers were still hard laborers involved in some grueling work that sent most of them to early graves. People who say that hard work is good for you haven't grown up in that world. Quite a number of people I knew growing up were missing an eye or a finger, and by the time they reached their sixties they had crooked backs and walked with limps. My kids have grown up in Florida and have had little contact with distant relatives, but I took two of them to my aunt's funeral a few years back (I generally avoid funerals). My daughter said to me, "Daddy, I've got three one-eyed cousins here!"

I grew up with no one who read for pleasure. Most of the adults around me read, at best, the newspaper, and then it was usually just the headlines. Despite that, I enjoyed reading the encyclopedia when I was small, and in high school I tried to write poetry—not because I had literary aspirations, but because I thought girls would like it.

DM: Were you a good student?

RC: I was indeed a good student, but I also cut up a great deal and played the class clown—again, trying to impress girls. I didn't get into serious trouble, just sent to the principal's office a few times. I knew that I had to study hard, because I wanted to go to college less out of a love for learning than a hope to escape.

DM: Was that desire how you came to writing fiction?

RC: As a senior in high school I took a literature class even though I wasn't interested in literature. It was taught by a young, bright teacher who'd not yet been jaded, and she really challenged us. One of the books she assigned was Faulkner's *As I Lay Dying*, and it changed my life. I had never read something in which the main characters were poor folk; I had always assumed that good literature was for and about the rich dogs, which it largely is. I thought, "These are my people!" and ever since I have sought out work by authors who write about real people, people who know what true struggles are, people who often do not know how they are going to pay their bills.

It wasn't until I read Walker Percy, though, that I started to have notions of becoming a novelist. I studied philosophy in graduate school, and Percy was a philosopher-novelist whose work I discovered as a senior in college. Throughout graduate school I made notes for a future novel that would combine philosophy and rural, poor folks. And, of course, professional wrestling.

DM: Were there other literary influences when you began writing seriously?

RC: I'm still influenced by the same writers: Mark Twain, William Faulkner, Flannery O'Connor, Walker Percy. Later writers include Harry Crews, Barry Hannah, and Padgett Powell. Oddly enough, what inspired me to sit down and bang out my first novel was Salman Rushdie's *The Moor's Last Sigh.* It was the first book I picked up by Rushdie, I had so much fun reading that novel that I was convinced that writing had to be just as fun. I'd written plenty of other stuff by then, all philosophy—a book, a number of essays in philosophical journals—and I figured that fiction had to be less tedious than that stuff. Less tedious yes, but far more difficult in another sense. I'm glad that Rushdie pushed me into doing the work, but I sure had no idea what I was in for!

DM: That's an interesting comparison. Something about it reminds of the distinction some make with the rivalry of small presses vs. big presses. There seems to be this distinction that what comes out of the former is serious writing, while what comes out of the latter is popular. How true do you think this is regarding fiction and poetry?

RC: That's mostly true. Big presses get big from selling many books. You can do that primarily by publishing pabulum. How many times can you pick up a novel from a big publishing house and read about another upper-middle class New Yorker needing therapy because somebody hurt their precious feelings or they're worried that Daddy might cut them out of the will? Some small presses publish junk, too, but even the junk tends to be adventurous or about a segment of the population not represented on the best seller lists.

DM: Should serious artists have the responsibility to be entertaining, or moral, or difficult, or any of these things?

RC: If you want people to read your work, you must be foremost entertaining—spin a good yarn, be funny, pull surprises, whatever it takes. I don't think you should be just entertaining. Nor do I think artists should be moral. When they try, they usually end up preachy and embarrassing. Artists have the responsibilities, I think, to shoot for excellence—which can sometimes be accomplished just by doing something different—and to show the audience something they may not have noticed before about their own experiences or social structure. This is often accomplished by making the audience uncomfortable or even shocking them. Some readers, for example, are turned off and even nauseated by the brutality in Cormac McCarthy's work, but he is a genius in the chances he takes and his eye for features of our lives that we would rather ignore. In the end perhaps the most important duty of a writer is to create interesting sentences. Nothing makes me want to continue to read someone's work than to find a sentence that demands that I reread it and try to unravel how the writer pulled it off.

DM: A lot of the reviews of your novel Purple Jesus *point out how multi-faceted it is and I agree. The reader can enter the novel from any angle: plot, character, culture, philosophy, etc. So when you write, how do you start out? Is it with one of these elements initially?*

RC: I start out with the main characters in mind. I want to have their personalities, troubles, and goals clearly in view before I start a novel. I keep a list of their traits, phrases they may favor, habits, etc. I also have the first and last scenes vividly imagined. That's what tends to keep me on track when I'm writing and get tempted to take a detour. I have a fairly complete outline by the time I sit down to it. When something from my notes gets incorporated in the work, I cross that out in my pocket journal.

DM: As a writer of fiction, is there anything wrong with relying too much on a writer's own life?

RC: Not a bit. After all, what else do you have? Even if you write a novel about a culture or time period that is not your own, as I did with *Gospel of the Twin*, despite all the research into that foreign culture and era, you cannot inhabit those characters without injecting them with your own experiences. When someone reads my work and asks, "Is this really about you?" my reaction is usually, "What do you care? Did you enjoy it or not?"

DM: What aspect of fiction did you have the most trouble with developing early on?

RC: I try hard to give each character a distinctive voice. One of the toughest challenges writers face is to keep their characters from sounding (and that includes internal monologues) alike, and usually like the writer him- or herself. I probably spend more time worrying about dialogue than any other aspect of my fiction, and not so much because they have regional dialects, but because I want their personalities to emerge from their speech patterns. I've learned a great deal about that from Barry Hannah and Padgett Powell.

DM: *I want to go back* to Purple Jesus *for a minute. There is vulnerability in some of the male characters in that novel, while Martha seems to handle violence and anxiety better, to a certain extent. Do you think women are better at handling these aspects of life?*

RC: In some ways, yes. Women are socialized with certain emotional expectations that men are taught to ignore or deny. When faced with challenges, men sometimes find that their traditional upbringing hasn't prepared them. In Martha's case, she had a horrid childhood from which she learned that she would not sanely survive unless she hardened herself and pursued her own goals relentlessly. Far too often in our society a young woman is taught that someday her prince will come, and Martha learned the hard way how dangerous that view can be.

DM: How important to you is the ego?

RC: If you mean, "Do writers have to be egotists?" then I suspect yes. The assumption that intelligent people will be willing to set aside hours of their time to read something you simply made up is damn well arrogant.

DM: Have you learned anything from other arts?

RC: Sometimes when I write a scene, I try to imagine it as a painter might. Perhaps I think of a violent scene illuminated like the tenebrism of a Caravaggio, or another with the crowded, swirling composition of an El Greco. I am more inspired by music, though. I often have a song caroming in my head that sets the tone of what I'm writing. It may be just a line of lyrics or a couple of measures of a melody. Other times a song seems to capture the overall mood of the entire book. For example, as I wrote *Purple Jesus*, I often thought of Robert Earl Keen's "For Love," which is about desperate, violent acts done in the name of love. I've entertained myself with thinking of the soundtracks for my novels if they were films, and I imagine Keen's "For Love" playing over the closing credits of *Purple Jesus*. That or maybe Bob Seger's

"Beautiful Losers," a title I'd steal if Leonard Cohen didn't already have a novel by that title.

DM: Do you believe in God?

RC: Careful when you ask a philosopher that question. The short answer is no; the long answer is not quite. The God of classical theism who is omniscient, omnipotent, omnibenevolent, eternal, etcetera I find an incoherent concept. Any one of those qualities, upon close examination, crumbles into absurdity. On the other hand, I find process theology, as expressed by Alfred North Whitehead and Charles Hartshorne, somewhat attractive. That God, one that is something like the consciousness of an organismic universe, however, is not the God of religion. This process view is expressed by some of my novels' characters. So, although I'm not religious, I'm deeply intrigued by religions and by theological questions. Struggling with religion is a central theme in my novels.

DM: What would you say to a young writer who wishes to write philosophical fiction?

RC: Lie down until the feeling passes. Far too many novels are deemed philosophical because some whiny character asked, "What's it all mean?" I put more direct philosophy into my work, sometimes outright naming the thinker whose idea I am treating and at other times including it more subtly. Part of what I want to do is to show that poor people lead lives just as complex as any of the more wealthy characters in popular fiction and that formal philosophy can express and clarify those issues. Trying to answer the big questions—Does God exist? Do we have free will? What is consciousness?—is better left to philosophers.

DM: What are your thoughts on Kierkegaard's Either/Or *or Nietzsche's* Thus Spoke Zarathustra, *then? They seem to handle these ideas in a narrative better than fiction writers.*

RC: That's fiction only in the broadest sense that you have fictional characters. *Zarathustra* comes close to having a plot, but like all of Nietzsche's work, it is aphoristic and episodic. It is probably better thought of as a series of vignettes connected by a common character. Both Kierkegaard and Nietzsche were marvelously inventive writers who went about doing philosophy in non-traditional ways. They are the intellectual grandparents of later thinkers who were more adept at fiction, such as Sartre and Camus.

DM: What was the worst advice you've ever gotten?

RC: Write every day. If you make a living solely by writing, either as a journalist or a pusher of bad writing, then perhaps that would be good advice. For most writers, though, I think it probably only causes stress.

If you're not producing much, you may worry that you've "lost it." On the other end, equally bad advice is to let the Muse speak through you. Waiting around for a mythical goddess to provide your creativity is like waiting for Bigfoot to reveal the secrets of the universe.

DM: It used to be a common supposition that writers who shared the same kind of content, or writers who were often grouped together by critics had a lot of communication with each other—I'm thinking of the "Lost Generation" as the most famous. Do you communicate often with other writers you see similarities with—guys like Eric Miles Williamson, Joe Haske, Patrick Finn?

RC: Yes, through email and phone calls especially with Williamson. He's been ceaseless in an effort to make sure that his "redneck mafia" makes connections to support each other in a literary climate that doesn't favor the sort of work we do. We admire and learn from each other's work and, perhaps most importantly, take heart knowing that we're from varied backgrounds—none rich, though—from all regions of the country. That regional spread, however, is a drawback, because we cannot get together as much as we'd like. When a number of us who belong to this mutual admiration club got together at the NoirCon 2014 Conference, we had a blast. Some of us had met a couple of the others, but no one had met everyone.

We're trying to scheme up other ways to weasel into conferences together. Just knowing that others are out there who share my literary concerns, and corresponding with them, does a great deal for helping me to keep the faith.

Rolando Hinojosa-Smith

Mexican-American literature has always been a kind of curiosity to me. I never tried comparing it to the Western canon. Instead I had always considered them different, not better or weaker than the other but simply different. While working through my undergraduate degree I became familiar with most of the major works in the Western canon and I also had a chance to read many of the major works in the Mexican-American canon. Rolando Hinojosa-Smith's work never appeared in any of the reading lists I got from Mexican-American professors. In fact, the only time I ever saw his name on a reading list was when I approached Eric Williamson about novels I should read by contemporary American authors.

I met Hinojosa-Smith for the first time while I was an editorial assistant at *American Book Review*. He came to deliver a lecture for the *ABR Reading Series* in 2010. He was touted as a kind of Chicano Faulkner for his play with narrative and point of view, but I never read his books as being purely imitative of Faulkner. Instead, I had always taken Hinojosa-Smith's work as being a challenge or response to the overly political nature of Chicano literature at the time.

When I first contacted Hinojosa-Smith for these interviews, about four years had passed since I had last spoken to him in 2010. He didn't remember me; I should have expected as much. I am sure I didn't have as much of an influence on his life at the time. But he was still as direct as I remembered him. His thoughts on most of the things I asked in the interviews are to the point, he is not one to waste his breath. For example, when I asked how he came to center his work around the Rio Grande Valley—his birth place—his answer was: "Writers know what they are going to write about; how it comes out is another matter."

This type of blunt response is not necessarily the answer that an interviewer asks for. But it is revealing in that it comes from a writer who is confident in the work that he has produced and will continue to produce. He sees a lot of things, with the exception of his work, as a triviality, something not to fuss over.

I like to think that in the decades to come Hinojosa-Smith will have a much more prominent place in Mexican-American literature—higher even than Gloria Anzaldua and Sandra Cisneros. Hinojosa-Smith's work takes risks that almost no other Mexican-American writer, with the exception of Stephen Gutierrez, has taken. Now whether those risks are always successful is another question. But it is precisely those risks that further the genre of Mexican-American literature away from its often melodramatic state or social-political preoccupations. Hinojosa-Smith knows, and those few academic critics that have considered his work know that, valuable literature is art. In the end Hinojosa-Smith's work will live on because of dedication to furthering the aesthetic possibilities of Mexican-American fiction.

Rolando Hinojosa-Smith's books include, *Korean Love Songs* (Justa, 1978), *The Valley* (Ypsilanti-Bilingual, 1983), *Dear Rafe* (Arte Público, 1985), *Klail City* (Arte Público, 1987), *Becky and her Friends*, (Arte Público, 1990), and *We Happy Few* (Arte Público Press, 2006).

DM: Your work is full of various types of characters, and many of them get a chance to narrate the events of the novel, or at least tell them from a different perspective. How would you describe yourself? What do you think you are like compared to all of the characters in your work?

Rolando Hinojosa-Smith (RHS): In regard to the characters and me, I try as much as any writer not to identify with the characters, however, every writer I've known and read always has a little something of one in the conversations. Not always, but (and only once in a while) a writer will have something of himself in the writing. Too much of it would spoil the narrative; what is being written is not an autobiography, that's why it's called fiction.

DM: How do you know when you are done with a work?

RHS: I've not thought on this and do not do so while I'm writing. Since the narrative and the conversions move forward, there comes a time (it's not a formula) when the end develops almost by itself. If the ending doesn't make sense, then the writer knows there is more to write and to develop. If the ending reads right, then that's it, you've come to the end.

DM: Well, after you've reached the end, how much revision is involved afterwards?

RHS: Revision. One writes, and one adds words or deletes them; it's an ongoing process. I then go chapter by chapter and see what's been left in and what's been omitted. If I'm comfortable with what I've done, I'll type a clean copy and send it in. I'm not sure that revision is the proper term for fiction because that would mean a change in the plot, in the characters, and, in some places, the setting.

DM: Do you think your work has influenced either the Mexican-American or American literary environment?

RHS: I've no idea if I've influenced anyone. That's not my role; I leave that to the reader. In February of this year, the National Book Critics Circle awarded me the Ivan Landorf Lifetime Achievement Award in New York City. That announcement made many papers in the U.S. and produced a number of interviews. I don't know how many read the articles, but it's not important. Why? Because the award was given and recognized by book critics from all over the United States. And, they did it by voting. Millions knew of it and millions did not. For a writer to worry about this is a waste of time.

Was I pleased? Very much so.

Since there are so many cultures in the United State, it's a waste of a writer's time to try to influence everyone or anyone. Every reader has his opinions, and, for a writer to worry over this is a waste of time.

I know I'll be read by professors and students (as the main audience) and not so much by the general reader. That, by the way, is the least of my worries, if I even have worries. I'm going to write and then it's up to the publisher to accept the work or to reject it. If the manuscript is accepted, fine; if it's rejected, fine. If a person cannot stand rejection that person is not a writer.

DM: Do you think novelists have the power to influence the culture in America beyond the academy?

RHS: The role of novels is always the same, to show a world as seen by the writer, as experienced (with certain changes) by the writer and to hold whatever it is that the writer holds as his truths, viewpoints, etcetera.

DM: What is the role of novels then?

RHS: Novels can entertain, illuminate, educate, but all in a moderate way. Before I write and when I'm writing, I don't think of this. I want what I write to be read by serious readers, and that's who reads the work.

DM: Your work has focused on a particular part of our country: the Texas Rio Grande Valley. Was this what you had initially set out to do? Did you know this even before you finished your first work?

RHS: Most writers write about the place they know like Heinrich Böll writes about Cologne for the most part, Faulkner set his work in Mississippi, Sinclair Lewis, the Midwest, Steinbeck wrote about what was happening in the United States during the time he wrote, and on, and on. Writers know what they are going to write about; how it comes out is another matter.

DM: Was there ever a central theme when you started writing?

RHS: Every novel has many themes, some are important to some readers, others are not; some themes hit the mark of a special group, and this may go unperceived by other readers. I know who will read my work in the majority and I try to write as well and as accurately as I can. If parts of history appear, then it must be covered faithfully. Since I'm not writing propaganda, I have to be accurate. If there is some comedy in the work, it must be fun to the reader.

DM: You have achieved a kind of success that is unique to Mexican-American writers. Your work is studied in academia by Chicano theorists, cultural theorists, post-modern theorists, and literary theorists. When you decided to begin writing seriously did you ever have any doubt that your work would get this attention in the face of a publishing market that is dominated by white authors?

RHS: Writing is a serious matter, and it always has been for me, for my parents and everybody in my family. As for criticism, that is not my role, I'm a writer, not a critic. Critics have their roles and their roles are important, but this does not concern me.

DM: What do you want your legacy to be?

RHS: I haven't given it a thought. Who knows what readers and critics will say twenty years from now? Arte Público Press has just published the first two novels I wrote; the novels appear in a bilingual edition, *The Valley/Estampas del Valle* and *Klail City/Klail City y sus alrededores.* How many critics, or professors, you for example, know that *Klail City* was published in East Berlin and then that Germany's most prestigious publisher (Suhrkamp) published it in Frankfurt or that Osnabruck University published

Korean Love Songs in English with a fine translation in German by professor Wolfgang Karrer, or that UNAM (Mexico City) published *Klail City*, and so on.

Pleased? Of course, who wouldn't be?

DM: What do you think is the most important element of fiction for a writer?

RHS: There are three important elements: the characters, the plot and the setting. They have equal importance.

DM: Were any of the three hard for you to master when you first started writing?

RHS: I started writing in the eighth grade at Mercedes Junior High. A one-sheet publication with writing on both sides. I wrote most of it. Ms. Alma P. Whatley chose who would be published, and that was it. More importantly, one must address the matter of reading: I come from a family of readers. My two sisters and my two brothers read at home as did my parents. Added to which, our parents read to each other. I also wrote during high school; not for the school, but for me. The first piece I wrote covered one incident during the Mexican Revolution of 1910; I was spending my summers in Arteaga, Coahuila, and one day, in Mercedes, at home, I wrote of two farm laborers returning from the fields when they are to be levied by a cavalry patrol. They attempt to escape and both are killed. I lost it, my mother found it, and I lost it again. I've not rewritten it, but I carry it in my head.

DM: Has writing become easier for you now that you have done so much?

RHS: Writing is not easy, and it hasn't become easier for me. I need to have the usual: characters, a plot and a setting, just like any writer. You've not asked, but writing, at times, is fun. You are inventing something that no one else has done before.

DM: So you have these three things when you start out. After that do you go straight ahead from beginning to end?

RHS: I go from chapter to chapter, and, during the writing, other ideas come to mind, and I will use them in the following chapter or later. I've always found it helpful to write from chapter to chapter. It's a matter of continuity.

DM: How important are our country's current social and political issues for your writing?

RHS: Social and political issues are inescapable. Those are the two chief ingredients in a novel. The novel may include humor (that, too, is inescapable), but the characters are alive, and they form a part of society.

DM: In an interview Faulkner once said of writers that, "All of us failed to match our dream of perfection." Concerning yourself, would you agree with that?

RHS: Yes, I've read much of Faulkner. My favorite is this one which my students write on the first day of fiction writing class: Read. Read. Read. Read everything—trash, classics, good and bad, and see how they do it. Just like a carpenter who works as an apprentice and studies the master.

Read! You'll absorb it.

Then write. If it's good, you'll find out. If it's not, throw it out the window.

JD Smith

JD Smith's books include the collection *The Hypothetical Landscape* (Quarterly Review of Literature Poetry Series, 1999), *Labor Day at Venice Beach* (Cherry Grove, 2012) and the essay collection *Dowsing and Science* (Texas Review Press, 2011). In *Dowsing and Science,* Smith touches on a wide variety of topics that are important to this collection. His concern for aesthetics, art, the working-class, and contemporary literature's relationship with the post-modern are all discussed in great detail in *Dowsing and Science.* What one appreciates most in Smith's work is its expansiveness and its energy. Near the end of "The Postmodern Smirk," an essay that considers the influence of the post-modern in every aspect of our society, as well as the art world's attempt—and in some cases failure—to move beyond it, we read: "They've left the rest of us something to do, to keep Pound's news that stays new, and show its permutations in a changing cultural landscape."

Smith shares many of the same working-class issues with the other writers in this collection. Though his work is not often considered working-class, his upbringing and viewpoints show a great concern for theories that inform such a designation. Smith grew up in the kind of working-class family many of the other writers in this collection have. Further, in interviewing him I found that his artistic, political, and social concerns are quite complex—another attribute he shares with these writers. Smith's answers to all of my questions were wonderfully insightful. For example, when asked about the irony of a label like working-class artist his answer was: "[We] know money is not enough to make a life, but we also know the bills aren't going to pay themselves," thus elaborating on an aspect of the working-class author that is not very often discussed by reviewers or the artists themselves.

When I had first read Smith's essay collection years ago upon its publication I was struck by its accessibility. *Dowsing and Science*'s subject matter is often handled by others in such a highly intellectual way that it is too inaccessible by a larger audience, this is often the case of the essays of William Gass or Jonathon Franzen. But Smith's work discusses any of its subjects in a way that is clear and without the residue of critical theory that many of our best intellectuals cannot seem to ward off. When I first began assembling this collection, Smith was one of the people I wanted to talk with because I was curious as to how he viewed such terms as working-class, contemporary fiction, and other things, such as book reviewing in the Internet Age. Smith provided a unique insight into all of these questions as well as others.

DM: In your first essay from Dowsing and Science *you write, "Other real worlds may exist, but the most common is the one that is contrasted to, or excludes, the academic and artistic worlds," and later, "[the real world] serves as a refuge of, if not scoundrels, the narrow and the unimaginative, lazy outside of commerce, who would have others join them."*

How do contemporary working-class authors situate themselves in this "real world" you describe?

JD Smith (JS): I can extrapolate from [Eric] Williamson's work. I can also draw a little on my own experience. It isn't as gritty as that of the authors, but I've had a fairly good ringside seat for grit. Both of my parents grew up with very little, and the shadow of the Great Depression still fell across the generations. Fortunately for them and for me they took advantage of a window of social mobility that is all but shut these days. People from modest backgrounds who become authors are usually beyond basic survival needs and have acquired enough intellectual curiosity to go beyond whatever is slopped into the popular culture trough, but they are also haunted by what Barbara Ehrenreich called "fear of falling." They—we—know money is not enough to make a life, but we also know the bills aren't going to pay themselves; likewise, we run into people at different points in the income spectrum who look at activities and their results only in terms of monetary value. This makes for an uneasy fit with both native backgrounds and the literary world, or any world that is primarily white collar and college-educated. My go-to reference on this experience is *Limbo: Blue-Collar Roots, White-Collar Dreams* by Alfred Lubrano, a first-generation college student who ended up going to Columbia Journalism School. My wife is the third generation of her family to go to college, and once I became aware of Lubrano's book I read it quickly myself and then made sure to put it in front of her.

DM: John Gardner once said of his novels and of all fiction that was moral: "Always I'm using the tool of language to dig a hole." And of those who are less concerned with understanding human morals: "Other people sometimes use the tool of language to chew on." Do you think it is still appropriate to look at contemporary fiction in this way?

JS: Notions of morality and utility in fiction—or any work of literature—raise more than a few questions. Didactic literature is tough to pull off—I can't do it—and it largely shouldn't be done. Any form of art should delight as well as instruct, and those functions should largely overlap. As for any system of morality or belief, I favor Flannery O'Connor's idea that the writer's underlying worldview should serve as the lens through which reality is seen and not as an explicit polemical position. In practice, any given work of literature lies somewhere on a continuum between instruction and delight, and individual writers' canons could be placed on that continuum as well. I once read of someone making a distinction between prophets and esthetes, though that should not be considered a black-and-white proposition.

DM: You've written in a number of different forms. Would you say that they inform each other? Is there a similar aim or aesthetic that you see yourself trying to achieve with all of them?

JS: Writing in different forms provides me a set of options I would not otherwise have. Until my late twenties I thought of myself almost exclusively as a poet, possibly to avoid typing more than necessary, but I ended up writing a lot of bad poems that shouldn't have been poems at all. Once I made my peace with that understanding I started engaging more seriously with essays, fiction and drama, which complement rather than inform each other. It's a relief to have options. At this point I usually know fairly early on what something is supposed to be: a free verse or formal poem, an essay, drama, self-consciously literary fiction or genre fiction, which for me almost always means neo-noir.

My aesthetic aims vary wildly across those categories. I am certainly a man playing the mug's game that Eliot described, trying to find an audience at one or another level of culture. If I were more prolific, and if branding were a larger part of my life, it would make sense to write under a different name in each genre, but so far that would lead to what would look like several guys with a few publications each. At any rate, I don't want to be a brand. I want to be an industry.

DM: One of the major debates in contemporary literature is the rise of blog-critics and online reviewers. Of course we are all aware of reviewers on Amazon and Goodreads, but there have been successful review sites like Rain Taxi and Full Stop. Do you think online reviewers are a good thing for literature?

JS: As Italo Svevo's Zeno said of life in general, the rise of online reviewers is neither good nor bad, only original. Distinctions in quality of reviewing emerge pretty quickly, even among short customer reviews on Amazon, let alone elsewhere. It becomes second nature to filter out ax-grinding, aggressive ignorance and the vague, unsupported assessments that sound like a grade school book report written at the last minute. People who clearly put work into online reviewing are picking up a lot of slack for the steep decline in column inches of newspaper reviewing, much of which automatically goes to big publishers' releases. *Bookslut* comes to mind in this regard, and so does the *Los Angeles Review of Books.*

DM: Critics like Laura Miller have urged against negative reviews with the idea that they really do no good to the general reader and the literary atmo-

sphere. Is it better to give attention to only good books? Is there any use for negative criticism?

JS: Time is the harshest critic of all. It renders a lot of negative reviews unnecessary, since work that is obviously bad from the start has a way of being forgotten—if it was ever widely known to begin with. In the moment, though, negative reviews are needed to stake out or maintain standards, and they can prevent any single school of art or criticism from becoming the only game in town.

Like hot sauce, though, negative reviews have to be applied with care. Using amateurs or obscure larval artists for target practice to show off the reviewer's wit and self-proclaimed superiority strikes me as cruel and more than a little cowardly—the original form of trolling. I am still amazed, and not in a good way, at Blake Gopnik's 2004 review of an unjuried art show in Washington. Who knows how many careers or even lives have been ruined by that review or others like it? In a place the size of D.C. he could have ignored the event and found something else to cover.

This still leaves at least a couple of very important uses for the negative review. One is to take down unduly inflated reputations and keep groupthink in check. Another is to call out dabblers who have made their reputation in other fields—or have the right parents—and want to shill a book as what someone once called a celebrity fetish object.

DM: One of my favorite essays from Dowsing and Science *is "The Postmodern Smirk." Can you talk about how this one came about?*

JS: The essay came about in the 1990s, a time when everything in the cultural atmosphere seemed to be ironic and otherwise reasonable people were maintaining that everything had been done before and all that remained was pastiche and fromage—in short, art about art. In 1997, when I was still teaching, one of my composition students self-mockingly expressed her fears about coming up with an idea for a paper by saying "It's all been done before." This was also the time the world's leaders were considering what to do with the "peace dividend" before they squandered it, and plenty of people were taking seriously Francis Fukuyama's idea of the end of history. In short, the relatively comfortable artistic and chattering classes mistook a comfortable lull for the new normal and didn't expect to face new challenges to our resilience and sensibilities. That very temporary luxury, which must have rightly looked preposterous to most of the world's population, was taken away from even those fortunate few on September 11, 2001.

DM: You bring up two interesting points in that essay, let me see if I understand them: on one hand you believe that much contemporary work—whether critical or creative—is merely a poor response or even a poor usurpation of previous works of the modern era, and the other idea is that there is still much to be done in the arts in regard to the results of things like social globalization.

Do you think there are any writers or artists that are doing any of these things now?

JS: You have definitely understood my points. As for the first, a lot of that is still going on, unfortunately, especially in the visual arts world (e.g., the money-driven fuckery of major shows and galleries), though some of that looks like a jet set adaptation of Poe's "The Masque of the Red Death."

My second point has largely and fortunately been invalidated by many artists' work—in all media—over the last fifteen years or so. I'm no expert in this field, but it seems that many painters have returned to realism to contend with an increasingly fantastical world. Some of the contemporary painters shown in the pages of *American Arts Quarterly* come to mind in this regard. Plenty of musicians are addressing social globalization by choosing from a vast palette of cultures and technologies, or avoidance of technology. Björk's solo career offers an obvious example. In literature any number of writers are now considering globalization and its discontents and working outside of the academic boxes of exclusively national literatures or of discrete lines of influence. I'll take the low-hanging fruit here and hold up as an example Junot Díaz.

DM: Who are your favorite poets?

JS: I always freeze up when I get this question. The answer depends on the mood I'm in and who I've been reading lately. I generally go for poets with quieter voices, the Dickinsons, Mandelstams, and Machados of the world rather than the Whitmans, Mayakovskys, and Lorcas. I'm continually amazed at the poetry from Central and Eastern Europe that emerged during the Communist era and somehow got published, then translated. I know none of the region's languages, but the clarity and authority of so many of those poets comes through in English.

Among twentieth century American poets my top choices would include Edwin Arlington Robinson, Weldon Kees, James Wright, and Sylvia Plath. What brings them together in my head is anybody's guess. As for living American poets, I am always interested in what Charles Simic is doing, and I am appreciating Kay Ryan more and more over time. Only in the last couple of years have I come to know the work of Jane Hirshfield, who finds ways to write intelligently about nature. I would also put in a word for Joshua Mehigan, who achieves a very Robinsonian combination of formal mastery and everyday speech.

DM: A lot of writers and critics say that poetry is a dead form. If this is the case why are there still so many poets? And do you think literary fiction is headed in that direction?

JS: The death of poetry sounds like the death of the novel or the death of the author or the idea that everything has already been done. I don't buy it. To the extent that poetry or fiction might not seem vital, that may speak to the lack of vitality of cultural institutions and gatekeepers. Some periods are more interesting than others, and some styles and movements hit dead ends, but let's not bury verse alive. That anyone can claim the authority to make such a statement also strikes me as odd. Who can genuinely keep track of all the poetry that's out there? Some still-unknown genius might just be starting out in a basement in Omaha. Song and story are integral to the human condition, and sometimes songs and stories need to be made for and about the present moment. If relatively few succeed, it has always been thus.

DM: What about essayists? Who do you go back to often?

JS: I haven't yet entered a phase of major rereading, which I would like to blame on my salaryman work life but probably should blame on my own distractibility and sloth. That said, there are essayists whose work sticks in my mind and can fairly be said to haunt me. E.M. Cioran comes to mind. "Against Utopia" presents a ground-level critique of the ideological waves of the last century, and that sense of humility in the face of the world at large offers a more humane way to conduct life and policy than the various programs that are driving politics and culture at the moment. Muddle doesn't appeal to our sense of the heroic, but it beats the hell out of Crusades, violent jihad, reckless structural adjustment plans and the resurgence of fascism in Europe.

Susan Sontag sticks with me as well. This sounds strange to me, too. My background and life could hardly be more different from hers. If I look for anything in common it is that both of us are/were English-speaking Americans. Still, her insistence on the primacy of art over criticism provided a valuable antidote to the theory-heavy thinking of her time. Though some works of criticism may be somehow better than many given works of literature, the "best" novel or poem will always be better than the best criticism of that work or any other. If I remember correctly, she describes criticism as the revenge of intellect on art—presumably for not being able to make art. Of course, I take issue with her thinking on other points. I need to stop procrastinating and write a contemporary response to "Notes on 'Camp.'"

DM: A lot of the other writers in this collection express disappointment with what has been characterized as the east coast publishing establishment that continues to print Updike derivatives. What do you have to say about the state of literary fiction in this regard?

JS: I probably can't add much to that discussion

besides agreement. The range of writers for whom mainstream literary success is available seems narrow in terms of personal and academic background, and the themes and settings portrayed seems narrow as well. If that weren't enough, people in a lot of fiction out there don't really do anything or have much done to them. Not that many molecules get moved aside from breath in a beach house or something.

To concretize this a little, I am reminded of a story I recently started reading in *The New Yorker*, which I subscribe to for the cartoons and Anthony Lane's movie reviews. By the middle of the first column someone had walked into a room with a basket of "courgettes." I'm of an age and level of interest in food that I already knew courgettes meant little squash—and I'll eat the hell out of some courgettes, which can be pretty tasty and tender if they're done right—but I didn't acquire that knowledge until I was in the second half of my forties. You don't have to be Bakhtin to know that this word choice indicated the story was by, for, and about a very narrow slice of the American population. I didn't finish the story. This speaks to the larger disconnect between academic and publishing culture and potential readers who are left out in the cold. Voices outside of a certain range of geography and class break into the slicks and the handful of big publishers—Donald Ray Pollock and my fellow Aurora, Illinois native Thom Jones come to mind—but this happens as a function of large numbers or a minor miracle.

DM: Are you very political?

JS: I work about three blocks from the White House, and I have no more influence than a shepherd in Nevada. There are several reasons for this. First, I don't have the temperament or force of personality for political activism, nor do I have the connections that would give me entrée into certain circles. Second, though I have given money to a couple of political campaigns in the last decade, my means don't put me anywhere near membership in the donor class. None of this prevents me from voting, though. I'm not going to forfeit the minuscule amount of power I have.

My political engagement usually comes out in inconspicuous ways like how I spend and consume, and in attempting to be humane and civil in my dealings with others. In a city like Washington more than a few people are not really interested in acknowledging the humanity of those on the far side of one or another race or class line, and I try not to perpetuate that problem. My political sensibilities sometimes come out in my writing as well, though not in the didactic preaching to the choir that infects open mikes and even scheduled readings. I am more interested in examining the assumptions implicit in political choices at all levels of society and sometimes holding them up in comparison to an ideal of how things could or should look if we had different aspirations. It's been a while since I've read Heaney's *The Redress of Poetry*, but his indirect approach is what I have in mind. Some of the poems I've had in issues of *Dark Mountain*, *New Verse News* and elsewhere may provide an idea of this.

DM: You maintain a different professional life compared to most of the writers in this collection. Can you talk about that?

JS: I'm a poor man's Wallace Stevens or Philip Larkin. Whereas they had support staff, I am support staff. I work as an editor and writer in the research department of an international organization in D.C. Most of my job involves helping economists make sense. Many of the people whose work I edit are native speakers of Spanish writing in English, and I am English speaker whose second language is Spanish. Part of the time I am figuring out what people are trying to say and rephrasing their thoughts in idiomatic English, and other times I am wrangling transitions and figuring out where sentences and paragraphs should begin and end; there is also a fair amount of straightening out the formatting of bibliographies and filling in their gaps. The writing I do involves minutes of meetings and presentations, newsletter articles and social media pieces that attempt to convey our researchers' ideas to non-specialists. I have to emphasize that none of this involves classified information or a security clearance. When I was younger and trying out different options I ran into a wall in applying to several government agencies (State Department, Peace

Corps, CIA) because at that time they weren't interested in hiring anybody who had been treated for depression. That may have changed by now, but by now my blog comments alone would probably disqualify me from a lot of jobs.

DM: What's it like being associated with non-literary people in this kind of professional life?

JS: For the most part I work alone and self-directed, so my associations are fairly limited. I actively dislike meetings and don't always play well with others, so this may be for the best. Most people in my department know I write, but that part of my life comes up only now and then. A few years ago one of our economists was kind enough to help arrange a reading of my children's book at his son's school, and I'd like to think everyone had a good time. It would be uncomfortable for everyone, though, if I called attention to what I was working on and publishing—or not getting published. That's at the heart of who I am, but it's not what they pay me for.

DM: Have you ever thought of teaching college/university as a profession?

JS: Absolutely. If I'd really understood my strengths and weaknesses earlier in life I might have planned specifically for that kind of career and never looked back. I value the intellectual stimulation and possibilities of recognition that academic life offers and the possibility of helping people now and then.

Then again, all choice is error. An academic life would have kept me from having some of the experiences that inform my writing, and from having a certain amount of humility and character beaten into me whether I wanted it or not.

I also would have run the risk of becoming one more victim of the deterioration of academia, and there are far too many already. I can barely handle being a horrified bystander as I hear and read about what happens as adjuncts and even tenured faculty are treated like widgets now that academia has been infected by business consultancy jargon and education is being treated as a commodity or service rather than a form of social infrastructure that needs continual maintenance.

In the previous decade I thought about moving back into academia, but until I get a windfall or retire from my current gig there is no place in it for me. At this stage of life I can't afford it, and even if I could I am too old (fifty-one) to start the tenure-seeking process, to the extent that tenure-track jobs even exist anymore. There is also an ethical problem: any adjunct teaching I would consider in retirement might take work away from somebody who needs the work and income more. Besides, the certification requirements work against me. When I finished at Houston in 1989 the program awarded only the M.A. and not the M.F.A, and almost all the relevant jobs out there require the M.F.A., if not Ph.D. preferred. So I now find myself with published books in three genres and an NEA grant, but ineligible for many jobs because of the lack of a terminal degree. At this point going back to school for the letter F would represent a bad career move.

DM: The small presses, in many ways, are tied to the universities. But even if they aren't, there is still a kind of academic atmosphere to most things "literary"—an example would be AWP. How does someone not in academics go about getting numerous books published and also continue to be aware of current intellectual debates?

JS: Knowing people in academia from my student days, and meeting up with more at AWP and other events, has certainly helped. I've gradually gotten a sense of the kind of work different people and presses are looking for. I also try to be easy to work with. As they would say in polling, my negatives are low among most demographics.

The overall structure of my life also helps. We don't have children, so that simplifies things a lot. (I am not one of those tiresome "child-free" people, though. Children are entertaining and I am good around them, but the way my life has played out I just don't happen to have any.) My job also has a generous number of vacation days, so that helps as well. I don't have any books forthcoming at the moment, so I have been a little wracked with self-doubt and wondering how well I am managing my time, but this could just be a losing streak that will be snapped, as I am currently circulating two poetry collections.

I'm probably a step or two behind people in academia on intellectual debates, but the slack in my schedule allows me to keep up reasonably well with at least the outlines of what is happening. Sometimes ignorance is bliss, though. Being outside of academia spares me from following the dust-ups and pissing matches that take place, especially online.

DM: What is AWP like for you?

JS: I find AWP overwhelming. I am an introvert with a high sensitivity to noise, and you can imagine what several days of social and sensory overstimulation does to me. By the end I am ready to lie down in a dark, quiet room for about a week. Still, I get to see more than a few people I wouldn't run into otherwise, and it's a pleasure to finally meet in person editors who have published my work. On the other hand, I am reminded of how small of a fish I am in the creative writing pond, and I have to fight my tendencies toward comparison and envy. My favorite AWP story is proposing to my then-girlfriend in Vancouver in 2005. She said yes, and we have been married for going on ten years. The timing was tricky though. I proposed on the day after we got there, March 31, because proposing on April Fool's Day didn't seem right. In 2004 the sight of casually dressed writers sprawled all over the lobby of Chicago's posh Palmer House, drinks in hand, amused me quite a bit.

DM: Can you talk about your association with the writers you associated with at NoirCon?

JS: I first have to say that my association with those writers is not as extensive as I would like it to be. I had a very good time talking with new friends and friends spread far and wide I get to see only on rare occasions.

In more concrete terms, almost all of my dealings at NoirCon flowed from my friendship with Eric Miles Williamson, whom I've known since 1986 when we were starting out in the Creative Writing Program at the University of Houston. He has been a big supporter of my work, especially my essays, and when he's edited my work for publication he has cared enough to encourage revisions, and he has shown me where I've simply gone awry at times, as in trying too hard to be funny or unnecessarily referring to popular culture in a book review. I've likewise seen a lot of his work in manuscript, which gives me a "there at the creation" kind of thrill when I've seen his published books. Eric was also my host on my first-ever trip to New York at the ridiculously late age of thiryt-four, and he introduced me to literary sites such as the Cedar Tavern and the Holiday Cocktail Lounge, both now closed.

As you can guess from those choices, there has also been a lot of hanging out and drinking, and to this day what Eric calls "phone cocktails" as we speak between South Texas and D.C. We spend more than a little time looking at our work lives from the perspective of first-generation college students who are still trying to figure out the tribal customs.

Through Eric I met Joe Haske a few years ago, and Joe has also taken a generous interest in my work, which he has run in *New Border* and *Sleipnir.* I only get to see Joe in person at events like NoirCon and AWP, and most of our dealings are by email. My loss.

The one NoirCon contact I can't trace through Eric is my friend and colleague, John Sandrolini, who attended only on Friday. I've known John since 1977, when my family moved to a house on the same street in Aurora, Illinois. His first novel, *One for Our Baby*—large portions of which are harder-boiled than a twenty-minute egg—came out in 2013. I read that manuscript as well, including some very early pages written by hand, and I recently read a draft of his follow-up novel.

Joseph Daniel Haske

Of all the novels written by these working-class authors, I have the closest relationship with Joseph D. Haske's *North Dixie Highway* (Texas Review Press, 2013). I had the pleasure of seeing the development of this book from some of its earliest stages up until its final manuscript. For about two years I typeset and designed the cover of the book. The final product of Haske's effort is a notable piece of contemporary fiction: it is written well, it is beautifully designed, and it is free of any grammatical errors—a feat difficult to achieve in many small press publications.

However, even if I had not designed or helped edit his novel, I would still hold the position that I do about *North Dixie Highway*; it is a work of high working-class realism. The novel shows that its author has learned well from his literary mentors Eric Miles Williamson, William Faulkner, James Joyce, and Saul Bellow. It also does well to challenge its predecessors. The realist camps of Raymond Carver and Ernest Hemingway often strived toward a working-class realism, but in the end created works that were void of character psychology and narrative depth.

There is a lot happening in Haske's novel and much of it is under the surface. For example, many of the hunting scenes in the novel are reminiscent of Faulkner's short stories. Reviewers have singled out "The Bear" as the most dominant of influence for Haske. I assume this comes from too much attention to surface plot devices. I would suggest, however, the short stories gathered in *The Vanquished*, where the young protagonists are presented as psychologically complex characters have much more of an effect on *North Dixie Highway*.

Many have pointed out that the main character, Buck Metzger's constant shifts in time are also nods to Faulkner and again I have to disagree. These shifts are more likely to be influenced by post-modern realists like Bellow. Though the novel's shifts are more restrained, the illustrations of Buck Metzger's anxieties are more aligned to those of Bellow's characters than any of those created by Faulkner.

The question for Haske now is: what will he do next. I like to believe that as good as *North Dixie Highway* is it must only be a primer for what the author is truly capable of producing. Haske is in good company. The fiction of his working-class peers is admirable. Almost none of them, however, have written a novel as their first effort. Further, almost none of them has produced a first work so well thought out that even its risks, upon close consideration, reveal themselves to be perfect fits into the novel's structure.

Williamson, Haske's mentor, may have initiated the melding of traditional Realism with high post-modernism in his works *Two-Up* and *Welcome to Oakland.* But if *North Dixie Highway* is an early indication of his potential as a novelist, it will likely be Haske who will see this working-class movement to its final incarnation.

DM: A reader can look over the American fiction of the past several decades and make the observation that there are certain things each time frame concerns itself with. The 1950's, for example, was concerned with a kind of ego-oriented fiction, whereas what followed it was the experimentation of the text—guys like Ronald Sukenick and Raymond Federman pushed this idea of the text being conscious of it being a text. Are there certain aesthetic or philosophical issues that you think a writer has to deal with today?

Joseph Daniel Haske (JDH): Well, egotism is still alive and well, for sure, but, the world completely changed in the past twenty years or so, with globalism, the prominence of the Internet, and an affinity toward social media and vir-tual reality. American society is more fragmented than ever, and despite the seemingly limitless access to in-formation and the potential for new ideas, popular culture seems to crave rehashed concepts with a small dose of simplistic, cosmetic tweaking. Sometimes I wonder if subtlety, nuance, and abstract reasoning in general have seen their better days. When I wrote *North Dixie Highway*, which leaves off in the mid-'90s, it really occurred to me how much different everything was then, and it really wasn't all that long ago.

DM: You had once said to me that for some readers the leaps in time and narrative you make in North Dixie Highway *may be difficult to accept. Why were they necessary for the novel, or rather, the main character? Do you suppose there could have been any other way to get the effect you desired?*

JDH: Without the leaps, *North Dixie Highway* might have been a doorstop—you know, one of those thousand-plus page books. The organization works because it gives the reader a better sense of the protagonist, Buck, showing how his mind operates and what he focuses on in some of the more stressful, intense moments of his life. The longer version could've been good, and it might conform to more readers' expectations of what a novel should be, but that's not the kind of book I set out to write.

DM: I think most readers' tastes are aligned with the traditional Realism of the 19th century. What makes contemporary Realism different? I ask this thinking of the accusation many experimental writers lodge against contemporary Realists—they claim Realism is an outmoded way of writing fiction.

JDH: Realism of the nineteenth century lacks the benefits of modern, post-modern, and contemporary insight. Some smug writers and critics tend to use the term loosely, pejoratively, for writing that doesn't look or feel as *avant-garde* as they think it should be. Whereas the Realism of the nineteenth century reacted against Romantic notions, the so-called "Realism" of the twenty-first century is sort of a catch-all phrase for writing that makes an attempt at verisimilitude, I suppose. You just asked me this question to piss me off, right?

If you look at superficial concerns, there's always that question of minimalism and its supposed correlation to progress. Contemporary "Realist" writers don't always blur the boundaries enough—try to make our prose look like poetry or whatever. I realize that some contemporary writers find this problematic. The conventional wisdom is that less is better, and there's certainly some truth to that, but I don't believe that less is always better, especially if it means we're obligated to whittle everything down so that it's more sparse and odd-looking than the post-modern experimentalists. Just because we don't go that route doesn't mean we're not aware of those writers. Hell, most of us owe a great deal to the post-modern experiment-talists and they inform our work much more than meets the eye, so don't dismiss our fiction because it doesn't look like prose poetry. When future readers and scholars look back at the great novels and stories of the twenty-first century, I think "Realist" writing, or whatever you want to call it, will be well represented in American literature anthologies.

DM: Today I think any reader or writer of literary fiction is aware of the many competing factions. Is it so bad that our country's literature doesn't have the kind of center we once thought we had?

JDH: The publishing industry has always been culpable on some level for ignoring work of significant artistic merit, particularly at the works' inception, but now things are worse: the big houses are even less charitable to literary writing than they have been in previous generations. It's an increasingly profit-driven/business-model approach, and our whole society is going in that direction. University and indie presses tend to step up and take chances with literary writers when the big presses decide to pass on their work, so there are still plenty of opportunities, but small presses usually aren't as well-funded, so getting the word out on promising new writers is another major obstruction.

It's easy to blame the publishing system, make it the scapegoat for all of our problems, but the truth is that the mess we're in is a whole lot more complicated. There are so many aspects of contemporary society that deserve blame for our problems, especially the general state of our educational system. Fewer and fewer potential readers seem to understand and appreciate aesthetics and they're seldom taught to grasp the connection between contemporary literature and the literary masterpieces of the past. Consumers simply tend to buy what the big houses are selling—it's just easier that way, to take other people's word for what constitutes great contemporary writing. So, on the one hand, there may be more opportunities than ever for writers to publish, but in a way, that leads to more apathy on the readers' part because there's a bigger shit pile to sift through if you want to find a few gems from the countless smaller presses, and the vicious cycle created by the large publishing house essentially dictates what occupies the shelves of major booksellers.

DM: In terms of contemporary readers, one would expect that there are at least a couple hundred thousand MFA graduates who can make these connections between work being written today and the great literature of the past.

JDH: These creative writing programs could be, and sometimes are, great for American letters, but do more harm than good when incompetent jackasses are at the helm. On the upside, these programs potentially help promising writers and keep literature alive by creating support networks and helping connect students and faculty with literary comrades. But, when creative writing students spend more time sitting around in a circle, stroking each other's egos or talking about feelings than they do contemplating the important questions, like, say, what makes great writing, that's where the problems start. Ideally, a program will encourage lively debates about aesthetics, about great works of literature, no matter how subjective faculty members believe these issues are. A great program prompts students to make their own discoveries and encourages individuality and idiosyncrasy rather than trying to create clones of their professors. Anecdotally, faculty across the country lament the nightmarish reality of thousands of "writers" coming out of creative writing programs who haven't read jack shit, but programs are forced to pass them on through, to keeps asses in the seats so the programs can stay afloat. That's such a bullshit concession and it serves as an argument against the utility of such programs if it's all true. No "writer" should dare produce a book until they've read at least a hundred great books and they've developed a thorough understanding, working through every detail, every aspect. The same way the best mechanics know engines inside and out, writers should know literature.

DM: How would you say your novel stands up in that great house of fiction? What great books does it rival, if any?

JDH: You know as well as I do that a writer isn't in the best position to make that call for so many reasons. It's a no-win situation. We'll have to leave any such speculation to the powers that be, esteemed critics, such as you, Mr. Mendoza, to decide.

Here's something I will tell you though: one of my goals for this novel was to write a better book about the place where I grew up than Hemingway did. People who know me best would tell you that I'm one of my own worst critics, and I certainly realize that any writer who claims to be completely satisfied with the final results of their work is either a complete fool or a damned liar. So, the boldest statement I'll make is that I know I can at least hold my own, and I'm not intimidated by any comparisons that people want to make.

DM: What was the most painful criticism you ever received?

JDH: It was so demoralizing I'd need a twelve pack and a good bottle of scotch or Kentucky bourbon to numb the pain. Got any?

DM: William Gass said that the best reason for writing was getting even, what's the best reason for writing for you?

JDH: Getting even, purging inner demons, finding kindred spirits—good company and that occasional free drink—these are all good reasons to write. The list of reasons not to write is longer, but the consensus seems to be that we can't help ourselves.

DM: Your work is often categorized as working-class, inherent in that designation is the political. Does a writer have a social responsibility towards his readers?

JDH: My gut response: fuck no. Too much politics can ruin art.

Then again, art without substance isn't worth much in the long run, is it? I lean more toward aesthetics than politics, and you might even say I'm irresponsible in that regard, or at least not always cognizant of the social impact my writing might have. Ultimately, though, a writer has to address the human condition in some way, whether consciously, conscientiously, or otherwise. I never blatantly manipulate anyone or impose my own judgment. I just put it all out there and let the reader draw conclusions.

DM: I know that you have written poetry, what do you find yourself carrying over from fiction when you sit down to write poems?

JDH: Attention to diction and detail, passion, intensity, musicality—I mean, as much as it's possible and reasonable to work these things into a novel. I'd consider most of my favorite novels poetic, or at least they aspire to poetry in a broader sense, so that's how I approach my writing when I'm working in any genre.

DM: Would you say that poetry is in a more difficult place than fiction is today?

JDH: I read some contemporary poetry, mostly because of my various editing positions. Art, in general, is in a difficult place in our society, but fewer people pay attention to poetry than fiction because introducing new poets to the world is almost never a profitable venture. If you operate a small press, you probably blow whatever advertising budget you have on the prose. Literary fiction is a slightly easier sell than poetry because there's always a chance that somebody might make a film out of a literary novel, bringing the press some much-needed cash. Aside from the work of canonical poets, most of the verse published on the big presses, I assume, are favors and potential tax write-offs. I could be wrong, but when's the last time you heard of someone trying to adapt a contemporary poem into a screenplay?

DM: Can you talk about your writing process?

JDH: You know, I really wish there was a specific process to talk about, life-altering secrets to share, but that's not the case. When I actually sit down to write, I've already thought about it all for a long time, and it's it in my head, or in notes that probably only I can understand. Then I'm tortured and frustrated by the ideas until I find the best way to deliver it in written form.

I've tried to work when I had a good buzz going, but for me, it doesn't usually play out well—the intensity goes sour too quickly: I drink too much and I get tired or ineffective. Drunk writing sounds cool, and most of us probably try it at some point, but in my experience, it's the most overrated part of the whole writer mythology.

At my best, I'm drinking coffee and there's moderate background noise to distract me from the surroundings. If the noise doesn't interfere with my focus, the music, chatter, or whatever, and if I'm not interrupted, I keep going, lose track of time until I run out of ideas or something or someone snaps me back into reality. I used to write more at night, but now my schedule forces me to find time whenever I can. When I'm in deep and somebody pulls me out before I'm ready, man, does it piss me off. I'm sure you know the feeling.

DM: What are your preoccupations?

JDH: Affection, immortality—do you really want the full list?

DM: Should a writer be forgiven for certain aspects of his work if the overall work has some kind of merit?

JDH: All great art succeeds because it fails beautifully. Consider the best novels, paintings, poems, whatever, and I dare you to argue otherwise.

Larry Fondation

Some who read the work of Larry Fondation notice that it is markedly different from anything they have ever read before. The work is a significant turn from the style of its literary predecessors, the post-modernists. In comparison to the working-class realists, there is something even more distinct. It isn't that Fondation's subject matter is different, but its prose matches so well to the characters in his novels that at times the reader becomes a participant in his novels more so than a reader of his novels.

Anxiety permeates Fondation's novels. It is the most familiar condition found in many of the characters. In the interview, a significant answer he had to my question about his prose was that in his appreciation of visual art, he wanted to blend the prose of his work as close to the content as he could. Fondation's attempt to capture a character at "the decisive moment"—he quotes artist Cartier-Bresson—is an acute observation of all of his works. There are other writers whose work is in a similar form, Lydia Davis is probably the most familiar, but no one else can claim the working-class subject matter as Fondation can.

Fondation was very interested in doing the interview. In addition to answering the questions, he sent me essays he had been asked to write for the French magazine *Transfuge*. I found his wide publication in France, like the work of Williamson, to be interesting. The French seem to have a taste for a particular kind of literary realism that portrays Americans as hard working, rough, and poor. In many ways, their interpretations of America are more acute than our own. I think one of the primary reasons Americans do not read much working-class fiction, at least that which is portrayed by the likes of those included in this interview collection, is because the mirror it holds up to reality is too true for them.

The literature that is read predominately today is escapist. It is no secret that people primarily read to be entertained, but it should be upsetting that that is the *only* reason our culture reads. As I said earlier, Fondation's prose is not characteristic of the majority of the working-class writers found in this text. Some may even use that as a reason to dislike his work. But I think Fondation is engaging with the context of his and his characters' situation in a unique way. This engagement asks the readers to become just as invested as the author and the text—perhaps in a way that is reminiscent of Beckett and Robbe-Grillet—and I find that to be a welcome invitation in American fiction. Some of Fondation's works include, *Angry Nights* (Fiction Collective 2, 1995), *Fish, Soap and Bonds* (Raw Dog Screaming Press, 2007), and *Martyrs and Holymen* (Raw Dog Screaming Press, 2013).

DM: I'll start with a question, that as a reader of your work for many years, has interested me almost from the outset: your work has a relationship with other writers in this collection, guys like Eric Miles Williamson, Ron Cooper, Patrick Finn, and others, to an extent that you all share similar subject matter that has sometimes been classified as working-class fiction.

But the form and structure of your work is very, very different. The length and sentence structure are perhaps the most obvious, there's a kind of compactness in your work that makes for an emotional density and anxiety.

Can you talk about your motivations for pursuing this form and how it developed?

Larry Fondation (LF): Urban life seems to me to be marked by a multitude of occurrences, of discontinuous incidents, and syncopated rhythms. Traditional narrative arc works well for certain kinds of portrayals—but not necessarily for the jumble of city living, especially living on or close to the streets. Indeed there are a lot of unintended consequences in contemporary life on both large and small scales. I try to approximate the discontinuity with short, stark vignettes that I hope, when taken together, add up to more than the sum of their parts.

I am also highly influenced by the visual arts. The photographer Henri Cartier-Bresson talked about capturing life at "the decisive moment." The idea is to evoke a broader, more complete story at a given moment in time—to imply the back-story. Of course, this leaves much to—in this case—the viewer's imagination; in my case, it would be the reader's.

If you look at Van Gogh's *The Potato Eaters* (1885), you see poor people eating a frugal meal. You can infer a whole story just looking at that one image. Van Gogh even talked about how the painting *smelled*—"not like paint," but "of bacon, smoke and potato steam." You can ponder the barkeep's entire life while looking at Manet's *A Bar at the Folies-Bergere* (1881). Even abstract painting goes for a sort of evocation. I think it would be great to be able partially to achieve that sort of effect and simultaneity in writing, to approach contemplating the whole thing at once. I am not saying I can do that, but I am striving towards it.

DM: For you there is a close connection between the form of your prose and contemporary life.

LF: Now, in the Internet era, the momentary is even more prevalent. One is able to Google craft beer one minute and the Emperor Justinian the next...that's life as it's lived now.

I'm not trying to succumb to "The Instant Society," where there is neither past nor future tense, because there are clear drawbacks and negatives there. But I'm not per se trying to critique it either, but rather perhaps to reflect it.

Formally, my fictional project is largely one of compression.

DM: Where does that leave meaning? Is meaning in your work—and here I'm talking about the didactic nature some see necessary in fiction—something that is highly important to you as you are producing a piece of fiction?

LF: In a word, yes. I believe in fiction about the world, not fiction in the living room.

DM: Tell me about your writing rituals? Do you have any?

LF: I work hard at my organizing job, which I love. So, not really. I write a lot in bars and cafes.

DM: What's the process like?

LF: I guess I am something of a collagist. I like to work with fragments.

DM: These collages or fragments, do they start with a singular image or idea?

LF: A student once asked Flannery O'Connor about her story "Good Country People." The student wanted to know when O'Connor knew the Bible salesman was going to steal Hulga's prosthetic leg. O'Connor replied: "When he stole it."

Most of the time, I write that way: I write one sentence, then another, then another, and so on. In my longer pieces—and some would say none of my work is long at all—I tend to have some sense of the shape of the work when I start. So, in *Fish, Soap and Bonds*, for example, I knew the end as soon as I started. I knew the book would end with Fish's death.

DM: Were you big on reading as a kid?

LF: I read a lot as a kid. I was both a bit of a punk-ass, growing up in a blue-collar neighborhood, *and* a nerd. I wrote in elementary school, and some in high school, but I didn't know any writers. And I didn't think I was smart enough to be a writer.

DM: What kind of authors were you reading then? Do you still read a lot of them now?

LF: Yes on both: Beckett. Borges. Cervantes, Kim Addonizio, Ron Sukenick, Melville, Hubert Selby, Flannery O'Connor, Genet, Guyotat, Richard Wright, Tillie Olsen, Nelson Algren, Dos Passos, Mary Robison, Vollmann, to name a few.

I remember my first reading of Hubert Selby's *Last Exit to Brooklyn*. It blew my mind. First of all, I grew up very blue collar. "Writer" was not on my list of possible vocations. Vocational schools were the sites of sheet metal shop and auto body repair practice. A college scholarship did help me get away from those kinds of professions, which I respect, but at which I suck. Then I read Selby. It was stunning to me that someone could write about the streets like that and in prose like that. Stylistically, I am not much like Selby but the whole subject matter and torrid prose! Wow! And, Samuel Beckett—all the "closed space" novels. So brief and beautiful and haunting.

And, in addition to the "very literary" stuff, I also have read a lot of Donald Goines and Iceberg Slim and all.

DM: Do you think that contemporary society has changed the way fiction can be written? Are writers thinking about this?

LF: I think the texture of contemporary society can change the definition of a novel (or, of fiction more broadly), but it hasn't much. Literature is one of the most tradition-bound of the arts. All sorts of things have been done in music and in the visual arts that are truly radical. Much less so in fiction. During the '60s and the '70s in the U.S.—the times of Barthelme, Sukenick, I think the form was becoming quite plastic. But not so much anymore—at least not here in this country. Most of what you find on the shelves of the big bookstores—to the extent that there are many left—could have been written in the nineteenth century. Now, that is not so true in Europe and other continents. Not so true with small, independent bookstores. And definitely not true in poetry today.

I do believe a number of writers now—Bett Williams, Hilton Als, Travis Jeppesen, to name just a few—are doing very interesting things formally.

I was asked by a French magazine, a couple of years ago, what I thought was the best novel about Los Angeles in the past twenty-five years, and I said NWA's *Straight Outta Compton.* I basically stand by that. My larger point is that rap and hip-hop can contain a great deal of narrative drive. Parallel in an odd way to Dylan and '60s folk music. A lot of good current storytelling is coming out in music.

DM: Would you consider your work experimental?

LF: I guess so. When pressed, I would say I'm an "experimental realist."

DM: In this sense, then, is the reader a kind of adversary?

LF: No, not at all. Despite the "experimental" tilt, my books are actually fairly easy to read.

DM: What are your opinions on the writer's commitment to politics?

LF: A few years ago, I answered a similar question for a forum published in the literary magazine *Fiction*

International. I don't think I can say it better now, so I will quote what I wrote for *FI* here:

> "Escapism is almost a national creed. We are all too often a country that retreats to our living rooms, televisions blaring, rather than protests in corporate boardrooms, bullhorns rallying the troops.
>
> In times of trouble, people frequently retreat to the intensely private when the public is too scary to behold. We may well be living in such a moment now.
>
> On the surface, artists and writers may seem to have a readier excuse for inaction than most—purveyors of beauty, guardians of the aesthetic gate and other effete bullshit. But, artists cannot afford that luxury. Artists must—at the very least—bear witness. I believe it is a moral imperative. To do otherwise is to be complicit. With the power of the "pulpit" comes concomitant responsibility. A clairvoyant who cannot say what he sees is no help at all. Some artists will protest that they just don't make that kind of art. Maybe they don't; maybe they can't. If not, then they should take to the streets. Doing nothing is not an option. Watching people go to hell in a bucket is almost as bad as sticking them in it as it descends."

DM: What is the biggest lie we tell ourselves?

LF: In October 2012, *The Economist* magazine published an article on inequality in the United States, entitled "For Richer, for Poorer:"

> "By counting the profits of capital, the share of national income going to the richest 1% has doubled since 1980, from 10 to 20%...Even more striking, the share amounts to 0.01% richest—about 16,000 families with an average income of $24 million—has quadrupled, from 1% to 5%..."

The lie: That the United States is a meritocracy.

Richard Burgin

I first came into contact with the work of Richard Burgin in a contemporary American fiction course. We didn't read any of it, but his works were on the reading list and the titles were intriguing. It would be about another semester until I bought *Shadow Traffic* (Johns Hopkins University Press, 2011) and *The Identity Club* (Ontario Review Press, 2005), but it would be a year or so before I would finally read them.

I was intimidated by the very idea of talking to Burgin. For one, he has to be the most successful of the group that I had interviewed, he is in many ways a literary statesmen not just for this group of writers but for contemporary literature in general. Burgin formed *Boulevard*, which is one of the best contemporary literary journals in the country—he regularly publishes work by people like Joyce Carol Oates and John Ashbery alongside talented newer writers. He has published two collections of interviews with Jorge Luis Borges and Issac Belshivis Singer, he is an accomplished composer, and then there is of course his fiction.

It was Burgin's many accomplishments that made me apprehensive to contact him for the interview. I thought, why would a man like this take the time to sit with me for an interview? I decided to read every Burgin interview I could find. When I was sure I had an original series of questions for him I sent an email inquiry. He returned with a phone call on the day after Christmas, I believe. I had missed the call, but I called back and we talked for a while about what one another was reading at the time. Weeks later, after the interview, he called again to simply tell me that he appreciated the questions I asked and that he would like to run an advertisement in the book when it was published. We would talk a few more times as the interview was being put together. He would inquire about Eric Miles Williamson and Joseph Haske, two people that we both know and whose writing and literary output he cared very much for.

It's really no doubt, to me, that Burgin is one of the great authors of our time. In reading the majority of his work I feel like his later story collections achieve a kind of aesthetic complexity that one rarely sees in the short story form. Perhaps his familiarity with various other art forms informs his writing—his music compositions are just as interesting as his fiction. It's a shame that many critics have not picked up on his work—or creative writing students for that matter. If either did I'm sure the world of literary fiction would be in a much better place.

DM: What do you think about the common obser-

vation that a writer's power fades as he/she grows older? I ask this thinking of the differences between your recent collections and older works like Man without Memory (1985). *In my opinion,* Shadow Traffic, *published in 2011, is much more dynamic in form and perhaps even content.*

Richard Burgin (RB): It's probably true that past a certain age, say seventy-five, the work of most writers, artists, and people in general begins to "fade" in power, but there are many glorious exceptions like Verdi, who wrote some of his greatest music in his late-'80s, such as his *Requiem*, and Matisse with his revolutionary cut outs he made right up until the end of his long life. As far as writers go it seems more difficult to think of examples of the best coming last, but they exist. (Dostoevsky published *The Brothers Karamazov* the year before he died.) In my case, though I am nowhere near the age of Verdi, I would also agree with you that *Shadow Traffic* is far superior in every respect to either of my first two collections, *Man Without Memory* and *Private Fame*. It was only with my third collection *Fear of Blue Skies* that my writing suddenly elevated in power, scope and, as you put it, "dynamism." Most of those stories in *Fear of Blue Skies* were written when I was about fifty years old. It seems that every writer has a period when they're at the top of their powers, only they don't know in advance when it will be (otherwise they could plan for it accordingly). It's like an invisible secret buried deep within your DNA that suddenly emerges. It's also in the nature of writers to always think they're at the top of their form. Only years later do they have a chance to realize when that time really was.

DM: With the growing rivalry of small presses vs. big presses there seems to be this distinction that what comes out of the former is serious writing, while what comes out of the latter is popular. How true do you think this is regarding fiction and poetry?

RB: My sense is that the vast majority of small press books of fiction and poetry attempt to be serious literature but that, in part, because big presses publish more books, the total number of "serious books" (even though it may be smaller percentage wise) is probably about the same. Let's remember that John Barth, Thomas Pynchon, William Gass, Issac Bashevis Singer, William Trevor, John Fowles, Alice Munro, Joyce Carol Oates, Saul Bellow, Ruth Stone, Herbert Morris, John Ashbery, and Louise Gluck were and are all published by major houses, and every one of them is as serious as they can be about creating artistic fiction, or poetry, regardless of what one might think of their efforts. There are also great writers like Jorge Luis Borges, and Samuel Beckett who were originally published by Grove Press, which is kind of a halfway house between a big and small press and writers like the masterful late Austrian Thomas Bernhard who was first published in the United States by the University of Chicago Press before being taken on by Knopf.

DM: Much of the commentary of your work has focused on aspects of violence, but I think you are working on other ideas, too. I don't necessarily see your work as being preoccupied with violence more so than it is attempting to address the complexity of the contemporary self, which is a self that does not have a singular identity or distinction.

RB: The world was even more racist and sexist than it is today, and while admittedly that made understanding people of color substantially more difficult, the majority of white Americans and British were undoubtedly less tortured by racial conflict, and more of them were also more sure of their religion with its comforting promise of an afterlife. It also seemed to be easier to judge people as good or evil then, which, of course, ties in with the notion of The Judgment Day.

In terms of real metaphysical truth, however, there's been a shift since Dickens and more people are less sure than ever about the origins and purpose of the universe. It seems we've reached a kind of philosophical impasse (beginning with Kant's *Critique of Pure Reason*) where we realize that we can never understand how the universe came into being because our minds have not been designed to be able to. Our brains, in other words, have been designed to comprehend things in terms of cause and effect, but that simply doesn't work when applied to the "objective" origin of the universe. To prove that, we have only to ask ourselves the question "how could there ever have been nothing, but how could there always have been something?" (Remember empty space is not nothing; empty space is simply "empty" space.)

The overwhelming number of writers of fiction and philosophy alike don't even attempt to answer or even dramatize this paradox. Jorge Luis Borges is an example of one writer who did, and that alone makes him one of the true geniuses in literary history.

DM: Are your writing hours pleasurable times for you?

RB: If I do it in the morning, first thing, before my lower back and leg pain kicks in and before I have to get my son to school, then my writing time is often deeply pleasurable for me. I have a number of stories coming out in good literary magazines and like every other writer, that helps my morale. They key thing is to do it as soon as I wake up because I think I do a kind of writing in my sleep, a kind of night writing or dream writing if you will. I want that night writing to carry over into my conscious writing. Writers are basically dreamers after all. I'm sure many others feel the same way as me.

DM: How much do the arrangement and the form of music shape your fiction?

RB: I grew up in a house of music. My parents were both child prodigy professional violinists—my mother was a soloist. My father was Concertmaster and associate conductor of the Boston Symphony. I always loved music more even than literature, but for various psychological reasons, I never studied music. However, I did compose over a hundred songs and piano pieces and a couple of my albums, *The Trouble with Love* and *Cold Ocean,* were very well reviewed and are now available on YouTube (among other places) in their entirety. But to answer your question directly, I don't think the arrangement and form of music has shaped my writings much. But living in a home of renowned professional musicians—all the musicians I met and heard about—did give me some valuable knowledge to write my first novel *Ghost Quartet*, which is largely set in the classical music world of New York and Tanglewood.

DM: Do you have any early memories from this time?

RB: Perhaps listening at the bottom of our first floor stairway—just out of eyesight, as my mother talked briefly to one of her students about me. The other contender was meeting my mother's mother and asking her why she had so many wrinkles. "Because I'm old," she said. Not the kind of transcendent memories one would have picked ideally and I can't be sure which was first. Childhood is a timeless kind of world anyway. In that sense it is also like a dream.

DM: What is the biggest lie we tell ourselves?

RB: Perhaps the deepest lie we tell ourselves is we believe that we understand how and why the world was created, and if we have the additional burden of being artists, that our best art (Shakespeare, Beethoven) will never be forgotten. Of course, everything will be forgotten eventually. "Art is the last illusion," my father once said to me, and for some years now I see that he was right.

DM: Did you have a lot of trouble developing your fiction early on?

RB: Probably in finding my own voice—no surprise there. At various times, depending on who my literary hero of the moment was, I tried to imitate Kafka, Faulkner, Hemingway, Borges, Beckett and the great Austrian writer Thomas Bernhard. Come to think of it, there were times when I was under the spell of Raymond Carver and Henry Miller as well. When you're a young writer or a reader of any age, it may be the only time when society encourages you to be promiscuous in your taste.

I might also add that because I began as a novelist and thought of myself primarily as a novelist for a long time (though I eventually published only two novels, *Ghost Quartet* and *Rivers Last Longer*) it was difficult for me to write very short stories. To this day, my stories tend to take place over a period of time, have character development and sometimes are told from multiple points of view. All features more associated with novels than short fiction. I think, sometimes, that some of my stories are almost like compressed novels.

DM: The first time I read your work was in a contemporary fiction undergraduate class with Eric Miles Williamson. On the surface your work appears to be working off of a realist model, but there is a kind of dynamic in the content of your fiction that I don't see often in contemporary realists. I think what I am trying to get at is that I believe you are experimenting with content for many of the same reasons that many contemporary writers experiment with form: to explore the self.

Can you talk about your experiences reading contemporary experimental writers, or whether or not they have had any influences on your work?

RB: I'm afraid I'm one of those who thinks that all good writing is experimental and that the term "experimental" as it is customarily used by academics and literary critics is a misnomer and essentially meaningless. Usually, it's applied to writers who construct their form or language in an unusual way like Joyce or Beckett. But then what are we to make of writers like Kafka and Borges, who write with such traditional clarity? Are they not equally original and experimental? Or what about a book like *Huckleberry Finn* or *Tropic of Cancer*? Weren't they also experimental? It also strikes me as odd that some kinds of "formal innovations" are considered experimental and others aren't. If I may be immodest for a moment, throughout my career I have written some short stories told from multiple points of view and have only read one other story by a writer who used the same technique, namely Robert Coover in his story "The Babysitter" (which I read years after my first multiple narrator story) yet few critics have ever labeled my stories as experimental. The truth is, words, like "experimental" and "avant garde" have no meaning in a world of infinite time. I mean, if time is infinite, what possible difference could it make to be ten or twenty years "ahead" of your time?

DM: Do you feel the same about those post-modern writers who many said were "experimenting" with the "text"?

RB: Was it really such a great discovery to realize that fiction is a text and life outside of literature isn't? The central philosophical issues of our time are the eternal questions that the overwhelming preponderance of writers never address, namely "given our metaphysical situation, how should we live"? This is what I want to read and write about, but of course to do so effectively is very difficult.

DM: Two post-modern writers, William Gass and John Gardner often debated about the aesthetic and moral responsibilities writers have to fiction. Do you side with either of these arguments? Do you think the artist has any aesthetic or moral responsibility?

RB: The artist's obligation is to make good art whether or not it has an overt political content. Many people feel that art is unavoidably political anyway. Everyone has as great a responsibility to behave ethically, not just artists. The writer's moral obligetions are no greater than anyone else's just because of his little gift for manipulating words.

DM: What can the goal of literary fiction be today given the kind of culture we live in?

RB: Isaac Bashevis Singer, with whom I had the good fortune to do a book of interviews, said that literature is essentially a form of entertainment. Jean Paul Sartre said that literature will replace religion. Personally, I think, at its best, its place is somewhere between the two.

DM: If it's okay for me to ask some technical questions, I'd like to know how you write out an essay or a story. Do you begin with an outline, sketches, drafts?

RB: I don't begin with an outline or sketch. I do

revise a lot as I'm writing and trying to move it forward. I have a general plot and theme in my head, but I leave plenty of room for spontaneous deviation from the plan on any given writing session. I guess it's kind of like improvising in jazz, or as I do in my own music and in that sense, to more fully answer one of your earlier questions, I guess my writing may be somewhat influenced by my experience with music.

DM: What do you think is the most difficult aspect of completing a work of fiction?

RB: To say something of interest and emotional power that only you could have written, a piece that takes root and flowers only on your own emotional real estate.

DM: You've done so much in your career. There are your interview collections, your music composition, Boulevard, *poetry and fiction. What do you want your legacy to be?*

RB: That I stayed essentially true to my vision as a writer and composer, and that I valued the pursuit of beauty far more than the pursuit of money or fame.

DM: Which of the works you've produced do you care most for?

RB: I think my best books are probably the story collections *Shadow Traffic* and *Fear of Blue Skies* and the novel *Ghost Quartet.* And, predictably, I think the collection I'm working on now is one of my best.

Jennifer Barnes

With the exception of Texas Review Press, Raw Dog Screaming Press is the major publisher of the writers included in this collection. They've published Eric Miles Williamson, Michael Gills, Larry Fondation, and George Williams. I met Jennifer Barnes, one of the founders and editors of the press while in Philadelphia. She and her husband had joined Gills and I for a few beers at a bar downtown. At the time it hadn't occurred to me to ask questions about the press. A couple of months later we had an email exchange about the interview collection and when asked if she would be interested in participating she agreed.

Today especially, there are groups of writers who cling to literary presses. As a reader I have always loved that I could walk into a bookstore, look for a pressmark, and know that I trusted the publisher's taste enough to buy a book from an unknown author. After high school, when I first began reading seriously, City Lights Pocket Poets, New Directions, Grove, and Black Sparrow were pressmarks that I looked out for. Later it was FC2, Cuneiform Press, Dalkey Archive, Texas Review, and of course, Raw Dog Screaming Press.

I assume most serious readers hold similar allegiances to other presses. For me, though, I have always chosen to read a particular press because, despite not knowing their philosophy for choosing the books they decide to publish, I believed a part of their reason was that they believed they were choosing books that follow in the tradition of great literature.

I was right with Raw Dog Screaming Press. Much of what Jennifer had to say rang true for me as a reader of her press. Raw Dog Screaming Press' reason for publishing many of their writers was their belief that they had something to write about. Barnes makes the observation that since "the ennui of the white upper-middle class has already been well-addressed," many small presses exist, and that many large presses use them as a kind of barometer to determine who the next big authors will be. The case of M. Glenn Taylor or more recently, Amelia Gray are good examples of this. Taylor's first novel, *The Ballad of Trenchmouth Taggart* had been on Vandalla Press but was later picked up by HarpersCollins. Gray's second novel won the Ronald Sukenick award by FC2; her later books were published by Macmillan/FSG.

Though both of these writers have produced work different from those included in this interview collection, I think that they, too, indicate the reading public's dissatisfaction with the big publishing world's preoccupation with the white upper middle-class. I am of course aware of the dichotomy that exists in the issue of the reading public. On one hand the majority of the reading public is likely to be upper middle-class and white, so this is a central reason literary authors like Jonathan Franzen, Jonathan Safran Foer, and those incarnations of them continue to be at the top of the major publishing houses. While working-class fiction authors very rarely end up in a major publishing house because, well, the poor don't read.

However, I think it's fair to say that the small presses have taken over innovation, and perhaps this has always been the case—White Rabbit Press is an early example of this. Contemporary publishers like Raw Dog Screaming Press not only look for aesthetically innovative texts, but are also not afraid of publishing texts that are politically incorrect, as is evident by their continued support of controversial authors like Fondation and Williamson.

The work of the small press publisher is very necessary in a publishing climate that makes it quite difficult for only a small amount of authors to see their work in print.

DM: Here is a good question to start with: Why of all the literary fiction being written in America do you choose to publish writers like Eric Miles Williamson, Larry Fondation, Michael Gills, and George Williams?

Jennifer Barnes (JB): There is a lot of excellent literary fiction being written and published in the U.S. right now, but while many authors of literary fiction are excellent writers a lot of them don't have anything to write ABOUT. The ennui of the white upper middle class has already been well addressed. Though I'd love to claim that we discovered Williams, Gills, Fondation, and Williamson we actually just lucked into them, but the minute I read the first page of Williamson's *Welcome to Oakland* I knew I chanced upon something magical with so much heart and essential realness that I couldn't pass it up. Of course these guys lie in their fiction, but they also tell the truest truth without political correctness or over-thinking. It's powerful stuff, and the literary scene needs it to stay vibrant.

DM: Can you talk about how these kinds of authors relate to Raw Dog's general aesthetic?

JB: Raw Dog Screaming Press was created to publish fiction that larger companies wouldn't touch with a ten-foot pole. Initially this meant to us genre books that mixed genres or had a literary sensibility. However, it actually covers a wide swath of excellent books, and the aforementioned authors certainly fit the bill. These authors are telling stories about the bottom-rung of society who don't read, don't buy books, and are quite often illiterate. It's not your usual Random House fare.

DM: From the perspective of a publisher, do you think the publishing business is in as much danger today as it was at other points in history?

JB: Yes, I'd definitely say the publishing business is in a dangerous place right now, possibly the most precarious position it's been in. But at the same time it's a period of many opportunities and possibilities. We've been pushing our way through such times for years now and looking back the danger was overstated but looking forward still seems as perilous as ever. But the fate of the publishing business is not inextricably linked with the fate of literature as many have often erroneously assumed. More people than ever are writing books, literature FOR the masses has become literature OF the masses. Is this good or bad? It's hard to say. Publishing has had to adapt to many changes in the past decade and will clearly have to continue to do so.

DM: Can you talk about how Raw Dog Screaming Press came into being? Were there particular reasons for starting the press?

JB: RDSP grew out of an online literary zine called *The Dream People*. After publishing short stories online for a few years we realized that there were many great books out there not being published because New York publishers had very narrow ideas about what could be published. With the new print-on-demand technology we realized we could change that.

DM: Do you have much contact with other small presses? Do you feel certain affinities with other presses?

JB: Being an indie publisher is pretty solitary. The publishing business is secretive about money and numbers. There is a certain amount of professional rivalry yet publishers love to talk about publishing and rarely get a chance to do so with people who can understand the minutiae. We were lucky to meet several publishers early on in our business who were happy to answer questions and have met many others over the years to admire. I've often wished for more chances to get together and share info, but publishers are also notoriously busy so there is not a lot of time for chit-chatting.

DM: Can you talk about your early interest in writing and what forms it took?

JB: I remember making a book of short stories for my father when I was in grade school, typing up each story and "binding" it with a construction paper cover. I also made a book of artwork. Even then it was about creating something larger, rather than simply about writing. In junior high I used to write horrible rhyming heavy metal lyrics, and eventually I wrote poetry and songs and played in a band. But for me these things have always been about collaborative efforts and putting together a larger project. I even organized a compilation CD with songs from fourteen local bands.

DM: Who do you think you owe your greatest debt to, as far sparking your interest in literature?

JB: I'd have to say that it was my mother reading books to me as a child that started me on an early path to being a bookworm, though I struggled to learn to read. Once I could read, however, nothing stopped me. I read the dictionary and all the questions in our Trivial Pursuit game. However, my sister got the same treatment and she doesn't read at all now, so it must have also been in my nature.

DM: Do you think independent presses have had much of an impact on the literary world of publishing?

JB: As far as I can see indie presses have the most influence on the literary world. They are the stew pot that larger publishers occasionally reach into to find the next big thing. Without the indie presses no one would bother to write indie lit at all.

DM: What kind of impressions have you made with the books that you have published?

JB: This is hard to say. Everyone has a different idea about what Raw Dog Screaming Press is or isn't.

Many times they think we've published books that we haven't published. We publish both genre and literary works, but some people think of us as a horror press, others as experimental or bizarro. It's all over the map. But I hope, and like to think, that we always maintain a reputation for being professional, exciting, and creative.

DM: Are you very involved in the actual printing, typesetting, and design aspect of the job? Is this something that you have always taken an interest in?

JB: Yes! In fact I have typeset most of the books and usually do the type for the covers though not the artwork. I am a trained graphic designer and would definitely be doing some kind of design even if I wasn't in publishing.

DM: Would you say that most writers are aware of how much other work it takes to get a book published and sold, besides the writing of the thing?

JB: I think most writers have a general idea that the submission process can be long and painful and that there's work involved. But the part they have very little actual knowledge of is the publishing process. To get a book written and published is work, but to make it a success is really hard work for many months, if not years! The single biggest change in the publishing landscape is that authors have more options and more responsibilities in the publishing process. If an author is not prepared to help with the marketing of their book it is unlikely to be a success, no matter which publishing route is taken.

DM: What has been the most difficult aspect of getting Raw Dog Screaming Press off and running?

JB: The hardest part of starting a press was definitely the business aspect, creating legal contracts, tracking royalties, and figuring out the taxes were all challenging. But harder than these things, and more difficult than starting a company, is keeping it going. In the beginning you're full of hopes and dreams and none of the drudge-work feels like work. But after years of doing it, another tax season, another royalty reporting period can make you wonder if it's worth continuing.

DM: What was the best kind of advice, or maybe the worst that you were given at the start of Raw Dog Screaming Press?

JB: The best advice we got was from Tom Monteleone of Borderlands Books who told us you just have to keep putting out more titles. This sounds simple, but it's the key to staying in business as a press. We did not receive any bad advice, but our biggest mistake was accepting returns and giving the typical large press discount of fifty-five percent. This was untenable at the level we were working at and almost put us out of business in the first few years.

DM: Do you think a lot of the work you publish would have otherwise been overlooked by major presses?

JB: I would say that the majority of our books would never be published if it wasn't for us or someone like us. We definitely take that into consideration when deciding what to publish. If we think a book would be widely marketable through a larger publisher we won't accept it and urge the author to submit elsewhere. That type of book would not do well at all on our press so it would be bad for everyone. I am proud to say, though, that some of our authors have been able to get major publishing deals after first being published with us.

DM: Can you talk about some of the unexpected things that have happened since you began publishing?

JB: We never expected to see our books reviewed in the *Washington Post* or receive starred reviews from *Publishers Weekly* and *Library Journal* or have our name mentioned in a *New York Times* article on the small press. We certainly never expected to publish a book of poetry by Till Lindemann from Rammstein or have one of our books get a blurb from actor Kurt Russell. It was quite a surprise to find that this year we have three books on the final ballot for the Bram Stoker award.

DM: Have eBooks had a significant impact on Raw Dog Screaming Press? Do you think it is something that is good for the culture or reading in general?

JB: EBooks have had a major impact on the industry and our press. We offer almost all our books in eBook format and have seen the distribution of sales go from five percent eBook to at least twenty-five percent. But I never bought into the idea that eBooks would replace print. There are both good and bad effects caused by the rise of eBooks, but I think inherently the technology is good and having a variety of ways to access and disseminate a text is good. However, it has certainly caused all sorts of problems that publishers will be dealing with for years to come.

DM: What are the other independent publishers and literary journals (print or online) that you admire?

JB: I admire any publisher that can stay afloat for more than a couple years! I've always been fascinated by the FC2 model and amazed that they have been around for decades. I've been impressed with Valancourt Books, a press that is putting out of print horror classics back into circulation at an astounding rate. Atticus Books is a literary press doing great work. Genre presses like Apex, Post-Mortem, and Grindhouse Press are putting out excellent releases, too, and I've been very interested in what Down & Out Books has been doing, including the *Stray Dogs* anthology.

DM: Design has always been an integral part of the book production. Though the content of literature is a much more important thing, a book's cover is how a lot of readers first become interested in an author/ novel. Can you talk about your design process, or maybe even an example from one of your authors?

JB: As a designer I take the cover of the book and even the interior layout pretty seriously since these are ways to clue your reader in to what's going on with the book. It's a bit like being a matchmaker to attract the right kind of reader. You want the book to find a good, appreciative audience. This is why we often use art that has already been created for our covers. It's a tricky process to try to explain to a visual artist what you want and have them create it. Every cover is different but we do try to involve the author and work together to come up with an idea. There are certain artists that we work with on a regular basis because we know they can create what we're looking for. For instance, our science fiction imprint, Dog Star Books, only uses covers designed by Bradley Sharp. Still, it's like anything else in publishing, sometimes all your thought and hard work pays off, and sometimes it doesn't, and it's hard to put a finger on why.

Stray Dogs Discussion Panel
AWP Conference, March 2016

About two years after NoirCon, Ron Cooper put together another panel for the Association of Writers and Writing Programs Conference. Cooper, Gills, Fondation, and Haske would participate on the panel; I would be panel moderator. If NoirCon provided exposure to Noir readers then AWP provided exposure to the literary crowd.

I would say that it was successful. One reason I am glad we went was we had the opportunity to meet a few other like-minded panels and writers. There were other great panels related to working-class writers that, had I previous knowledge of them, I would have loved to include in this book. When most readers think of working-class fiction, they ultimately think of male writers and sometimes *white* male writers. But, this conference proved that there are just as many female and minority writers who write working-class fiction.

It is something that I have tried to make a better effort at correcting in my own work as a critic. However, the larger machine has done such a great job of relegating each group to a specific literary section. There is no unified working-class writer's genre, but there are Chicano writers, female writers, LGBTQ writers, black writers, and so on. It is true, however, that many of these writers can just as well be working-class.

Stephen Gutierrez, who I did interview, was on a panel about working-class fiction in Southeast Los Angeles. Jodi Angel was on a panel about women and working-class fiction. Had there been enough time I would have loved to interview many of the writers I met at AWP but I suppose this desire will always be the case.

My central purpose in this panel was to ask questions that dealt with the working-class aesthetic and politics. This intent mirrored the panel at Noir Con, however, it did not end up being a repeat of it. Fondation provided a point of view that was different from the previous panel and this also provided a different kind of response from the others panelists as well. Overall, the panel was a success and I think it will serve as a touchstone of sorts in this group's history.

DM: How important are aesthetics and morals in fiction to you?

Joseph Daniel Haske (JDH): I don't set out to write a didactic kind of fiction with the scenes in these stories. Though, I try to stay true to the details and the people in the fiction. It's odd that we find a morality or a lesson in writing today. I wouldn't think of trying to include a moral, rather I'd prefer it to happen in an organic way.

DM: One of the more unique aspects of working-class fiction is its use of metaphor. As a writer it seems like the aesthetics of working-class fiction takes much more time to develop because as readers we don't often see these types of characters in the tradition and especially in mainstream literary fiction. If we can think of style in fiction as the way critic Daniel Green defines it: "when writers manipulate language for artistic effect," can you talk about how you have arrived at a distinct style?

Ron Cooper (RC): I do write about the people I grew up with. Most of these people were dirt poor. It would make no sense for me to have characters make descriptions or metaphors about things that didn't relate to them. For example, it wouldn't make sense to have one of my characters never talk about their house which had no wheels on it. In *Purple Jesus* there are a lot of metaphors which reference tools, something that the main character grew up around.

Of course the risk that you run is that if the majority of readers are used to reading work that is on the *New York Times* bestseller list compared to reading about poor people then they aren't going to understand what a feeler gauge is, or what I mean when I write that a character's house was built on a bevel.

DM: How do you feel about that risk?

RC: Well, I don't care. [audience laughs] I'm not sure that any of the people who are used to reading bestsellers would get through ten pages of my books. And I'm fine with it that way. Whatever the subject matter you're writing about has to have metaphors that reflect the lives of the characters. It has to be meaningful as far as showing what those characters are up to.

DM: All of the people on this panel have jobs that have allowed them to pull themselves out of the working-class environment. Michael, why still write about these characters in your fiction?

Michael Gills (MG): My wife asked me the same question earlier, right before she spilled wine all over our table. I told her, "Well, shit, what do you think? Do I get up in the morning and say, 'Goddamn, I'm gonna write me some working-class fiction.' [audience laughs] Do I say, 'Man, I'm gonna write me some white-trash stuff!"'

I don't know, Dan. This distinction between regular literary fiction and working-class fiction doesn't make no sense to me whatsoever. I don't even understand what it means. And I'm on the panel [audience laughs]. I see no distinction. Faulkner had these people called the Snopes's. Give me a break! That woman that laid down and slept where that dead man's skull had been all those years. All the rich kids are reading that story that begins, "My mother is a fish."

Working-class fiction, that's Faulkner, that's fine. But if Faulkner's working-class that means that the notion of the working-class breaks down. They'll be reading him as long as people are reading.

I don't see a distinction.

I grew up in Lonoke County, Arkansas. I never went to a dentist. I never knew anyone who had been to college, except for my teachers. They had been to college. I didn't get them. I got to college as an athlete; I walked on as a football player.

I took a workshop. I decided I was gonna be an English major, and my dad, who was a truck driver said, "English major, what the hell is that? You gonna go around being English!" [audience laughs] Somehow, I got into a writing workshop led by a man named Buddy Nordan, he wrote *Wolf Whistle, Sugar Among the Freaks,* and *The All-Girl Football Team.* I believe he is the best writer that ever lived and he was my workshop teacher. The first day of class he was drunk, and he got up to dance on the table. I looked at him and said, "Yeah, he's my kind of person." He was the kind of person I grew up with. I wrote this poem called "Night Dreams in Logic Class" about me sneaking down through a barbed wire fence in my backyard. I don't know if any of you ever snuck through a barbed wire fence, but you get one barb that catches you on the top of your back and when you let go of the barbed wire it makes this odd sound. I walked down to a barn and the moon was out. Sitting on a bale of straw was the dance teacher wrapped in a horse blanket. The moon was pouring in and forming slats on her white skin.

I wrote that down in a poem. I didn't know anything about line breaks, so I just put them wherever I thought they looked good. I gave it to Buddy and he said, "Oh my God! Michael, you're the one we've been waiting for!" [audience laughs] He marched me down Miller Williams at The Arkansas Press. He read my poem. I had this line in there that read, "Eyes of horses shone above the straw." But I was never a good typist, so he read "Eyes of hoses ..." He said, "Oh my God! Michael that's the finest phallic image I've ever seen." [audience laughs]

After that I had a one-point grade point average, but I was able to attend the Graduate Program at the University of Arkansas. How do I keep writing working-class fiction? Well, I don't know anything else.

DM: Larry, two recent articles appearing in The New Republic *and* Electric Literature *commented on the unpopularity of contemporary working-class fiction. They offer the thesis that working-class fiction does not offer the optimism that most readers want in contemporary fiction. What would be your response to this observation?*

Larry Fondation (LF): The moment that we're living in has this dominant narrative where we expect everything to end up hunky-dory at the end of stories. That certainly wasn't true in the '30s. Some of the things that Michael was talking about in regard to Faulkner speaks to that. *As I Lay Dying*, for example, is a novel about poverty and dying.

My writing is urban, not rural like my colleagues on the panel. Tom Kromer wrote a novel called *Waiting for Nothing*. It's an amazing novel, of course a lot of people today have never heard of it. But it was read during its own time. It's hard to see how we have gotten to this point in fiction.

One way would be to understand that we have this crazy search for optimism when people are more anxious than they were before. Also, I don't think people are organizing the way they were in the '30s. The sense of hope becomes a fictional hope that people search for in books.

Ron mentioned earlier that an MFA cost a shit load of money, but if you go to Europe people don't know what you're talking about "an MFA."

Originally we like to think that books are for the people, of the people, by the people. Now we have a lot of books that are for the rich, of the rich, by the rich. That's a factor.

It's also measured in critical circles. Most of the shit that is in the *New York Times-Book Review*, on the front page, is very thin. It's popular fiction in the guise of literary fiction as opposed to agreeing that literary fiction includes things like working-class fiction: the ninety-nine percent. It shouldn't just include Henry James and other books.

Finally, I think it's just where our appetite is. If Shakespeare hadn't written *Othello, King Lear,* and *Hamlet* and he only wrote shit like *The Merchant of Venice* he would be a minor playwright. Tragedy has a huge place, yet we seem to be hell bent on ignoring that.

We're drifting away from a sense of consciousness of class at all. There is this myth that we live in a classless society. We live in the most unequal society since the Robber Baron Era, yet we don't see a new resurgence of the labor organizing or a new United Farm Worker's movement. And we don't see an organized working-class fiction genre. I think it's all caught up in that.

DM: Ron, you want to add to that?

RC: I would like to respond to that. When I was in high school I hated literature. I never wanted to read; I think it was because my teachers hated it. My senior year, we had an honors class. We had one teacher who I think could and did read. [audience laughs]

She assigned *As I Lay Dying* and when I read that I was amazed. Here are my people! I was thinking, "You're allowed to write about them?" I didn't know that anybody could do that. That class really changed my life—Michael, it made me wish my mother was a fish. [audience laughs]

Reading that book made me feel like I had a duty to continue writing stories like that. Yes, Faulkner understood poor people, but he damn well didn't like them. I think many readers, even poor people, don't like to read about poor characters. It reminds them of how horrible life can be.

You know they work minimum wage for their whole life and there is no end in sight. These are the people that we write about, and it is hard to put a lot of hope in there. We try, but there isn't much to be hopeful for when you live like that.

I never went to a restaurant when I was younger. My mother and everyone I knew just said, "We're just poor people. If we showed up they could tell, they'd have us all arrested." There is a notion of shame about being poor. If you grew up like that, you don't want to be reminded. You'd rather read about characters that worry about their investments than characters who worry about pinworm.

LF: For me, that recognizable book was Hubert Selby's *Last Exit to Brooklyn.* As an urban person, I went "Oh hell, you can write about people who are way, way down and out?" Where I grew up, the people had fucked up lives. But you got to have an appreciation for that. Today we have lost the lesson that we can best understand a society by looking at its margins. You can understand more about the medieval concept of religion by looking at a monk's drawing in their illuminated manuscripts then by reading scripture. You go into the churches in Europe and there are these huge religious scenes on the ceilings and walls. There are visions of hell, bestiality, and orgies, and this is a cathedral. In the past people were more willing to grapple with social issues then we are now.

DM: The narratives of your work are also different than other writers who document the working-class.

JDH: Well, you know there is something Ron said about the lived experience. When my book came out someone asked my uncle if he read it. His answer was, "Read it?! Hell, I lived it!" The poor have no interest in reading at all.

A common aesthetic that we all have—which is different than writers before—is that we just jump into the stories. There are no buffers; no one is holding the reader's hand as the narrative moves along. That type of delivery can be arresting. If you look at regionalist authors in the nineteenth century you have an educated observer guiding you through these dark places so it isn't scary.

You know sometimes critics will suggest that the characters in our novels are illiterate, and they might think we are too. [audience laughs]

DM: What do you think about that Michael?

MG: Well, I'd like to disagree with what's been said. This fiction isn't anything to get down about. Our type of work is uplifting. As a matter of fact, Faulkner, in his speech on winning the Nobel Prize, he tells us our duty as writers. He says the main task is to move the reader; to uplift them. To me there are great moments of light in our lowest points. My African-American brothers and sisters call this "the blues," right? Blues is uplifting.

When my mother was put in a facility, I had the opportunity to live with people that were poorer than us. They were Cherokee Indians. The Trail of Tears went right across their front yard. They had no water or electricity in their house. But they got their water from the spring that flowed nearby. It was called Matrimony Spring because the water was so good that if you drank it you were married to that water for the rest of your life. They'd go up and bring it down in buckets. They watered their hog with the finest water I have ever tasted. I have never been around happier or more jubilant people.

These people were so poor. The men were construction workers and they would steal shingles from the job sites. Their roof was shingled with different colors so the roof looked like a patchwork blanket. They were the nicest people to be around even though things really sucked most of the time.

LF: I agree, these stories can be uplifting. But, for the record, I find *Waiting for Godot* uplifting. [audience laughs] You know, if I need a boost of energy, I'm going to read some Beckett. Beckett writes, "I can't go on. I'll go on," or "Fail again. Fail better." I agree with Michael, I'm not trying to romanticize the working-class. I don't find that content depressing. But my response to Dan's question was that other people find our work depressing. The greater half of our society finds working-class fiction depressing. I don't know that anyone who read the *Grapes of Wrath* in 1939 when it came out said, "Oh, how fucking depressing." But today people read the same kind of work and they have a different reaction to it.

The kind of work that makes me depressed is Henry James.

CONTRIBUTORS BIOS

JENNIFER BARNES is a co-founder of Raw Dog Screaming Press and has edited many of RDSP's titles, including a Penn Oakland award winner and two Bram Stoker Award winners. Her children's book, *Better Haunted Homes and Gardens*, illustrated by Kristen Margiotta, is a seasonal favorite. She is also an accomplished graphic designer.

RICHARD BURGIN'S nineteenth book and ninth collection of short fiction, *Don't Think*, was published in early 2016 by Johns Hopkins University Press. His stories have won five Pushcart Prizes and been reprinted in numerous anthologies including the *Best American Mystery Stories* and *The Ecco Anthology of Contemporary American Short Fiction.* He is the founder and editor of the literary magazine *Boulevard.*

RON COOPER was born and raised in South Carolina. He now lives in Ocala, Florida, where he teaches at the College of Central Florida. He has published philosophical essays, and is the author of *Heidegger and Whitehead: A Phenomenological Examination into the Intelligibility of Experience* (1993). His novels *Hume's Fork* (2007), *Purple Jesus* (2010) and *The Gospel of Twin* (2015) are available from Bancroft Press.

PATRICK MICHAEL FINN is the author of the novella *A Martyr for Suzy Kosasovich* and the story collection *From the Darkness Right Under Our Feet.* He lives in Arizona and teaches at Chandler-Gilbert Community College.

LARRY FONDATION is the author of five books of fiction, all set primarily in the Los Angeles inner city. Three of his books are illustrated by London-based artist Kate Ruth. He has written for publications as diverse as *Flaunt Magazine, Los Angeles Times, Fiction International* and *Harvard Business Review.* He is a recipient of a Christopher Isherwood Fiction Fellowship. In French translation, his work was nominated for SNCF's 2013 Prix du Polar.

MICHAEL GILLS' first collection of short fiction, *Why I Lie*, was published by University of Nevada Press in 2002. A novel, *Go Love*, came out in 2011 from Raw Dog Screaming Press. A second story collection, *The Death of Bonnie and Clyde*, was published by Texas Review Press in 2012. Gills is Associate Professor/Lecturer of Writing for the Honors College at the University of Utah. His collected papers are archived and available for research at the University of North Carolina at Greensboro.

STEPHEN D. GUTIERREZ is the author of *Elements, Live from Fresno y Los* and *The Mexican Man in His Backyard, Stories & Essays.* He is the winner of the Nilon Award from Fiction Collective II and the American Book Award. Originally from Los Angeles, he lives and teaches in the San Francisco Bay Area.

JOSEPH D. HASKE, former Chair of English at South Texas College in McAllen, was awarded the 2011*Boulevard* Emerging Writers award for short fiction. His work is featured in journals such as *Boulevard*, *Pleiades*, *The Texas Review*, *AleCart* and *Fiction International*. His novel, *North Dixie Highway* was published by Texas Review Press in 2013.

WILLIAM HASTINGS works as a farmhand and as a bookseller. He is the author of *The Hard Way* (Tiger Bark Press) and the editor of *Stray Dogs: Writing from the Other America*.

ROLANDO HINOJOSA-SMITH was born in Mercedes, Texas, on the 21st of January of 1929. Of the five sons and daughters, four chose teaching as a profession. Their mother, Carrie Effie Smith, taught school in a ranch in the Rio Grande Valley of Texas. Their father, Manuel G. Hinojosa, was a ranch hand, later, a policeman in a town of six thousand. He and Mrs. Hinojosa taught the five boys and girls to speak, read, and write Spanish and English at home. Each one skipped at least two grades during their public school years. Aside from the U.S., some of his work, in translation, has been published in France, Germany,

Mexico and Spain. He plans to retire from The University of Texas at Austin on August 31, 2016 as The Garwood Professor. He earned his doctorate at the University of Illinois.

DANIEL M. MENDOZA'S essays and reviews have been published in *Boulevard*, *American Book Review*, *Colorado Review*, *Texas Review*, and other places. He is an assistant editor for *Pleiades: A Journal of New Writing*. He lives in the Texas Rio Grande Valley.

JUAN OCHOA returned to the States after studying and practicing law in Mexico in the mid-nineties. Ochoa is the author of *Mariguano a Novel* (Texas Review Press), and his short fiction has appeared in *Analecta 37* (UT Austin), *The Rio Grande Review* (UTEP), and online at *Fried Chicken and Coffee*. Ochoa has been everything from pistolero to professor and is currently teaching freshman English at South Texas College in the Rio Grande Valley.

JD SMITH has published three collections of poetry, most recently *Labor Day at Venice Beach* (2012), and he has received a Fellowship in Poetry from the National Endowment for the Arts. His other books include the essay collection *Dowsing and Science* (2011), the humor collection *Notes of a Tourist on Planet Earth* (2013) and the children's picture book *The Best Mariachi in the World* (2008). He lives and works in Washington, D.C.

GEORGE WILLIAMS' essays and stories have appeared in *The Pushcart Prize*, *Boulevard* and *The Hopkins Review*, among others. He is the author of a novel, *Degenerate*, and three collections of stories, *Gardens of Earthly Delight*, *The Valley of Happiness* and *Inferno*. His novels, *The Goose Girl* and *Zoë*, are forthcoming.

ERIC MILES WILLIAMSON is author of three novels, a book of short fiction and three books of literary criticism. He has won many awards internationally, and his books have been published in the UK, Finland, France and Germany. He edits the *Texas Review*, *Boulevard* and *American Book Review*. He lives on what is called La Frontera, in South Texas, a dozen miles from the Rio Grande River.

OTHER TITLES FROM DOWN AND OUT BOOKS

See www.DownAndOutBooks.com for complete list

By J.L. Abramo
Catching Water in a Net
Clutching at Straws
Counting to Infinity
Gravesend
Chasing Charlie Chan
Circling the Runway
Brooklyn Justice

By Trey R. Barker
2,000 Miles to Open Road
Road Gig: A Novella
Exit Blood
Death is Not Forever
No Harder Prison

By Richard Barre
The Innocents
Bearing Secrets
Christmas Stories
The Ghosts of Morning
Blackheart Highway
Burning Moon
Echo Bay
Lost

By Eric Beetner (editor)
Unloaded

By Eric Beetner and
Frank Scalise
The Backlist
The Shortlist

By G.J. Brown
Falling

By Rob Brunet
Stinking Rich

By Mark Coggins
No Hard Feelings

By Frank De Blase
Pine Box for a Pin-Up
Busted Valentines
and Other Dark Delights
A Cougar's Kiss

By Les Edgerton
The Genuine, Imitation,
Plastic Kidnapping

By Jack Getze
Big Numbers
Big Money
Big Mojo
Big Shoes

By Richard Godwin
Wrong Crowd
Buffalo and Sour Mash

By William Hastings (editor)
Stray Dogs: Writing
from the Other America

(*)—Coming Soon

OTHER TITLES FROM DOWN AND OUT BOOKS

See www.DownAndOutBooks.com for complete list

By Jeffery Hess
Beachhead

By Matt Hilton
No Going Back
Rules of Honor
The Lawless Kind
The Devil's Anvil
No Safe Place (*)

By Jerry Kennealy
Screen Test
Polo's Long Shot (*)

By Ross Klavan, Tim O'Mara
and Charles Salzberg
Triple Shot

By Paul D. Marks and
Andrew McAleer (editor)
Coast to Coast vol. 1
Coast to Coast vol. 2 (*)

By Terrence McCauley
The Devil Dogs of Belleau Wood

By Bill Moody
Czechmate
The Man in Red Square
Solo Hand
The Death of a Tenor Man
The Sound of the Trumpet
Bird Lives!

By Gary Phillips
The Perpetrators
Scoundrels (Editor)
Treacherous
3 the Hard Way

By Tom Pitts
Hustle

By Robert J. Randisi
Upon My Soul
Souls of the Dead
Envy the Dead (*)

By Ryan Sayles
The Subtle Art of Brutality
Warpath

By John Shepphird
The Shill
Kill the Shill
Beware the Shill

James R. Tuck (editor)
Mama Tried vol. 1
Mama Tried vol. 2 (*)

By Lono Waiwaiole
Wiley's Lament
Wiley's Shuffle
Wiley's Refrain
Dark Paradise
Leon's Legacy (*)

(*)—Coming Soon

www.ingramcontent.com/pod-product-compliance
Lightning Source LLC
Chambersburg PA
CBHW050340190726
48284CB00007BB/2088

9781943402502